LIGHTSLEEP

First published in Great Britain 2006 by Matthew S. Batham

This edition published 2009 by Matthew S. Batham

LIGHTSLEEP

BY MATTHEW S. BATHAM

For Tom and Oliver Batham

CHAPTER ONE

Damon Dodge was a brat. He did bratty things like faking hysterical crying when his mother wouldn't buy him what he wanted and flicking bits from his nose into other people's dinners. He looked like a brat too. His face was round and pale – it rarely saw any sun – his nose was small and turned up like a pig's snout and his dark hair was always messy because every time his mother tried to comb it he threw a tantrum and broke the comb in half. It wasn't an ugly face exactly – on another, pleasanter child it could have looked okay. But Damon was thoroughly unpleasant and this seeped through into his features like a disfiguring poison.

He lived with his mother in a three-bedroom semi-detached house in a suburb of London called Ickrington. He didn't know his father, who had left home when he was a year old. There was only his mother to discipline him, or at least try to, in between working part-time as a secretary in an estate agents.

Damon took advantage of his mother. He knew she was too busy to notice all his hateful antics. Once, he had trampled on her vegetable patch, just for the fun of it. When his mother had come out to water her precious produce she had found a bed of mashed up cabbages and pulped potatoes. Damon denied everything. Another time he had deliberately blocked the lavatory bowl with tissue paper and wallpaper paste so that when his mother pressed the flush, water had poured all over the bathroom carpet. These are just two examples of the hundreds of brattish things Damon had done over the eleven years since his birth.

Damon, as you can imagine, was very unpopular at school. He was extremely proud of his reputation as a sneak, a bully and a dirty schemer. His cruel pranks ranged from placing a cockroach in the lunch box of a timid girl called Lucy Pollot – who had to be shaken before she would stop screaming – to spraying furniture polish on the classroom floor so that the teacher skidded and fell as she bid her pupils "Good morning".

The teacher, Mrs Hicks, had been taken to hospital with concussion, which Damon thought a great result.

The day on which Damon's real story begins was not a school day. It was a day during the summer holidays and Damon was bored from the moment he climbed reluctantly out of bed.

The table was laid ready for his breakfast when he stomped into the dining room. He complained about the type of cereal and said the milk was sour, before stomping to the living room to watch television. There was a programme on about a man who raced around America in an expensive car, being very nice to beautiful women and solving all sorts of mysteries. Damon didn't like him. He also wondered why his mother's car was so small and why she wasn't nearly as pretty as the women on the telly.

Soon Damon became bored again, and this meant his mind returned to plotting his next devilish scheme.

Because he was on holiday his mother had taken time off from her job. She was at home, but too busy catching up on housework to keep an eye on him every minute of the day. Damon could hear her washing up in the kitchen as he crept upstairs thinking: "What can I do to make her life more difficult?"

By the time he had reached the top of the stairs he had thought of something and it was an extremely wicked idea. Probably his nastiest yet.

In her bedroom, Damon's mother kept a box of matches. They were hidden in the drawer of a small bedside table. She used them to light a candle to read by at night because Damon had accidentally – or so he claimed – knocked the bedside lamp over and broken it. Damon knew the matches were there. He had found them one day when he was routing through his mother's room looking for Christmas presents.

"I'll start a fire," he was thinking. "A great big one which will burn the house down!"

As he stepped towards the side-table he tripped and landed heavily so that air rushed out of him with a whooshing sound and tears sprang into his eyes. He sat up rubbing his head, which hurt, even though he couldn't remember having hit it. His attention soon returned to the bedside cabinet and the small drawer that contained the matches.

Damon hadn't really meant to burn the house down. He had just wanted to start a small fire that he could stamp out quickly when his mother smelt the smoke. But matches are dangerous and fire has a life of its own. Damon took a match from the box and struck it. He stared at the flame with glee, fascinated by how something so small could cause so much damage. The flame crept down the match until it reached his fingers.

"Ouch!" Damon dropped the match and put his burnt fingers into his mouth, feeling angry.

A snake of flames weaved across the pink carpet. Damon screamed, which he knew was not a boyish thing to do, and leapt to his feet. The snake of fire had reached the bed and suddenly the quilt, which hung to the floor, was ablaze. Damon screamed again as the flames reached for the ceiling like great red ghosts.

There was no way he could reach the bedroom door – the flames had formed a hot, wavering barrier. Behind him was another door which led into a long thin room which ran along the side of the house. One side of the room sloped with the roof. His mother called it the 'long room'.

Damon pulled this door open and fell into the long room, choking, his face burning. He slammed the door closed to hold back the flames and black smoke. But the thin wood was no match for the horror Damon had created with one small match. Soon smoke was crawling underneath and the crack around the door began to glow red.

At the far end of the long room, where boxes of old toys and books were stacked, was a small hatch which opened into a dusty little room full of gurgling pipes and a tank full of water.

Damon ran towards it and as he ran he heard something strange. Someone seemed to be knocking on the door from the other side. Damon hesitated in front of the hatch, listening to the Tap! Tap! Tap! and wondered who could be hiding in the pipe room. He suddenly remembered, with a pang of horror, a picture he had seen in one of his mother's big books. It was a picture of Death tapping on the door of a house belonging to an old man covered in warts.

"Maybe this is Death come to take me away. Maybe I've burned to death in the fire," thought Damon, desperately.

"Open up!" came a high-pitched voice. It didn't sound like the voice of Death. Damon took a step backwards, his mouth open wide. But smoke was billowing down the room, curling around the boxes, sneaking up like a living creature.

"Open up!" came the voice again, and Damon pulled back the small bolt which fastened the hatch and flung it open. Sitting cross-legged on one of the water pipes was the weirdest little man Damon had ever seen.

He was tiny, shorter than Damon, with a large head like a melon. His eyes were wide and bright green, his nose so long it nearly touched his grinning mouth. He wore a green tunic and boots that curled at the ends. In his little pink hands he held a clipboard, which he glanced at before returning his gaze to Damon.

"Hello there." he greeted.

Damon stared, his mouth still hanging open.

"No time to be shocked," said the man.

Damon noticed that where the floor to the pipe room should have been there was a black hole which appeared to go on forever.

"Come in," said the man, beckoning.

"There' s no floor," stuttered Damon.

"Stand on the pipes, stand on the pipes," chirped the little man.

"It'll break," insisted Damon, looking doubtfully at the nearest rust-encrusted pipe.

"That's not important."

"It is to me!" Damon was regaining some of his usual brattyness.

"Fine," replied the man and he wrote something on the clipboard with what looked like an ordinary ballpoint pen.

"What are you writing?" demanded Damon.

"Sorry?" The man looked up, startled, as if he had forgotten Damon was there.

"What are you writing?"

"Damon Felix Dodge, burned alive in house fire," said the man.

He stood on his stubby legs, slipping the clipboard into a large pocket in the front of his tunic.

"Nice to meet you. Hope the flames lick you up quickly so there's not too much pain."

The man made to jump from his pipe.

"Wait!" Damon could feel the heat from the fire burn his back.

"Hurry then," snapped the man, his grin dropping into a frown.

Damon jumped onto the nearest pipe and the small door slammed shut behind him.

"Now jump," said the man.

"What?" Damon looked at the man as if he were mad.

"Jump!"

"Don't be stupid!"

The man shrugged and began to take the clipboard from his pocket.

"All right! All right!" said Damon. "But what's down there?"

He peered into the dark pit below them.

"You'll see," said the man, and he grabbed Damon by the arm and jumped into the abyss.

Damon screamed his loudest , longest scream of the day.

CHAPTER TWO

Falling wasn't the breathtaking experience Damon had expected. It was more like floating downwards than falling. He thought briefly of a book his mother had tried to read to him – something about a little girl and a rabbit. Damon had refused to listen past the first chapter. He didn't like little girls or rabbits.

Once he had recovered from the initial shock of being wrenched into space by the small man, he regained some of his usual arrogance. "Where exactly are we falling to?" he demanded.

"I'll tell you when we get there," replied the little man.

"Well I'll know then, won't I!" retorted Damon. He would have stamped his foot if there had been anything to stamp it on.

"Then stop wasting my time asking questions that will answer themselves in no time at all, you silly boy," said the dwarf – or whatever his companion was.

Damon didn't like being called silly. He wasn't used to people criticising him. The other children at school were too scared, and even his teachers were a little reticent about telling him off.

Bump!

They had reached the bottom of the hole.

Damon looked about him as he stood – the landing had forced him onto his bottom. He was surprised to find himself still in the room of pipes.

"Well here we are," said the little man, placing a large tick on his clipchart. "Safely delivered."

"We haven't gone anywhere," said Damon.

"That's sort of true, but not exactly," said the dwarf. "In some respects we've travelled an awfully long way, in some ways, we haven't gone anywhere at all."

"Oh, shut up!" Damon turned to glare at the little man, but he had gone, leaving just an acrid smell, like that left by a firework.

Damon shrugged and listened for the sound of flames from the adjoining room. Everything seemed peaceful. Perhaps he'd had an incredibly realistic dream. He pushed open the door and peered apprehensively into the long room. There was no evidence of fire or smoke and no sign that it had ever licked its way along the room.

"It really was just a dream," thought Damon, stunned by his own vivid imagination.

He walked, still in a dream-like haze, through the door that led to his mother's bedroom and again found no evidence of fire. But something was different – many things, in fact. There was a new unpleasant smell to the room, like clothes had been left in a damp pile to go musty, and as Damon looked around he saw other differences – the bed was covered by a thick, hairy, black blanket, the curtains were a dark, dusty grey and drawn against the daylight. The dressing

17

table had changed from a modern pine wood unit to a hulking, dark-wood monster with six connecting mirrors, all reflecting Damon's shocked, confused expression. His confusion increased when he saw the clothes he was wearing. His mother always dressed him in the best clothes she could afford, which of course were never good enough for Damon, but he would have been grateful for them now. Somehow his own clothes had disappeared and he was dressed in the tattiest brown jumper and the most shapeless grey trousers he had ever seen. He looked down at his feet and where his trendy white trainers should have been was a pair of scuffed old brown boots. But strangest of all was his face. It was his face, but altered ever so slightly, so slightly that only Damon himself would have seen the difference. The nose was more pointed and less snout-like, the cheeks more sunken as if he was in need of several good meals. Damon's stomach rumbled and he realised that for the first time in his life he felt genuinely hungry.

"Damon!" A voice full of hatred and anger called his name. It sounded slightly like his mother's voice, but she never spoke to him like that. "Damon get down here, now!"

Damon walked warily from the bedroom to the small landing and looked down the stairs at the owner of the wretched voice. It was his mother, but she had changed too.

"Get down here and help your sister clean out the stable."

The fact that Damon didn't have a sister seemed almost irrelevant compared to the creature that resembled his mother. She looked like the evil fairy from one of the silly books his real mother was always trying to read to him. Her hair was jet black, her face deathly white. She wore a long grey cardigan that reached to her ankles and clung to her waif-thin body like a nasty, itchy skin.

Damon descended the stairs with trepidation.

"Quickly!" the evil mother kept saying like a demented parrot. "And when you've finished cleaning out the stable, the main attic needs sweeping. Just sweep it, don't nose around up there. Remember what happened last time you and Wynne went snooping."

Damon didn't remember, of course. But then he didn't remember anything about this strange place, which resembled less and less the home he had just left. The carpets, which were bright and highly patterned in his house, were a dark, dirty grey here, as if the terrifying mother-creature liked to blend with her environment. The walls were bare brick and stone. In some places, where the cement had crumbled, sunlight filtered through, casting meagre light onto the dull floor.

Damon reached the bottom of the stairs where he was greeted with a sharp cuff across the head.

"Be quicker next time," hissed the evil mother-thing. "Now hurry up, Wynne's up to her knees in horse manure."

Damon didn't know which direction to hurry in, so stood looking perplexed.

"Now what's wrong?" demanded the evil mother, her icy blue eyes burning into his.

"I don't know where the stable is," said Damon.

"Don't be insolent!" Damon received another painful slap. He couldn't remember ever having been hit before. People just didn't hit him.

The evil mother twirled on the heels of her grey shoes and stormed into what in the real world would have been the dining room. Damon peered after her and gasped. More than anything, this room had changed. In the real world it was no more than twelve feet wide and not much longer. Here it was a great cavernous room, with bare stone walls like that of a castle. It seemed far too big to even fit into the house, the ceiling rose for at least forty feet, the corners decked with the faces of screaming gargoyles. The floor of the vast, cold room was covered in piles of huge, dusty books. One volume lay open near to the door and Damon tried to decipher some of the ancient-looking writing.

"Hurry up!" came the strident screech of the evil mother, and Damon turned to face the front door, that here was made of thick dark wood, not metal and glass. Suddenly it flew open and Damon gave a startled squeal, which made him extremely angry and embarrassed. A small girl with fair hair tied in a ponytail stomped into the hallway and glared at him, hands on hips. Judging from the filthy state of her grey dress and scuffed brown shoes, and the fact that she smelt of horses, Damon guessed this was his sister, Wynne.

"What's keeping you?" she demanded.

Someone else shouting at him!

Damon opened his mouth to protest at Wynne's tone of voice, but she had stomped back out of the house. Damon followed, annoyed, despite his anxious state. The driveway hadn't altered that much. It was still uneven and sprigs of grass were sprouting up between the cracked grey stone. However, from outside Damon saw that the only thing about the construction of the house that remained the same was that the front door was at the side, facing the front door of its neighbour. He stepped back staring aghast at the sprawling mass of turrets and spires that had moments ago been a simple semi-detached house in the London Borough of

Ickrington. It was a huge, dark monster, with smoke billowing like dragon breath from dozens of tottering chimneys that were dotted across a mass of grey slate roof. The tallest spire rose from the middle of the house and around its distant tip circled three bats, who obviously hadn't realised they were nocturnal animals. The house next door was an average-sized semi, just like in the real world.

"Damon, what are you staring at?" asked Wynne, irritably, waiting for him a short way up the driveway.

"It's huge," gasped Damon. "It's like a castle."

"What?" Wynne was scowling at him, but there was a note of concern in her voice.

"How did it get so big?"

Wynne edged a little closer to him. "Are you pretending to be mad to get out of helping me or something?"

"I've never seen anything like it," continued Damon, "It's like a witch's house."

"Damon," said Wynne, staring at him as if he were the most stupid person in the world. "It is a witch's house. Now stop acting the idiot and come and help me clean the stable!"

CHAPTER THREE

Damon followed behind Wynne, reeling from the latest revelation. Not only had his three-bedroom semi-detached home turned into a sprawling gothic mansion, but his mother had turned into a witch. Add to this the fact he had somehow acquired a bossy little sister and that the garage, which he was now approaching, had turned into a huge wooden stable, complete with farmyard smell and great brown horse, and confused barely began to sum up Damon's state of mind.

"You feed Barrow while I shovel out some of the muck, then you can sweep out some of the old straw," said Wynne, picking up a spade with a wide square head from the stable doorway.

Damon wanted to argue, but decided to wait until he understood more about what was happening to him. Unfortunately acting natural was difficult as he knew nothing about feeding horses. He guessed they must eat straw, otherwise why would there be so much of it lying around?

He drew some harsh strands from a bale just inside the stable and held them under Barrow's nose. The horse sniffed at them, managed a polite lick and then swung his great head from side to side and blew through his pouting black lips.

"Yuck!" Damon stepped back to avoid the spray of saliva.

"What's wrong with you?" asked Wynne, handing him a cloth bag with a long strap. Damon shrugged, seemed to remember seeing a film where a bag like this one was hung round a horse's neck, and so hooked it over Barrow's. The horse found the content far more tempting than the straw.

As Barrow fed noisily, Damon glanced around, taking in yet more dramatic changes.

Next to the stable was a low gate leading into a vast, overgrown garden – at least ten times as big as the garden he had left behind. The house that should have formed the other half to Damon's semi didn't exist here, nor, it seemed, did the busy road that had lain just beyond. Instead, rising all around the garden for as far as Damon could see, was a dense, towering forest.

"Damon, will you stop dreaming and start sweeping," said Wynne, pushing a broom into his hand.

"Sorry," mumbled Damon, a word he couldn't recall ever having used before. He gripped the end of the broom but kept staring at the forest. It rose steeply with the gradient of the ground beyond the garden, the branches tightly entwined like jungle vegetation.

"Damon!" Wynne's warning tone pushed him into action. He began half-heartedly to sweep the old straw onto the driveway. "Has mother been getting at you again, is that why you were hiding?" asked Wynne, depositing a spade-full of manure onto Damon's pile of straw,

"Maybe," said Damon, and so that he would not have to make conversation with his newfound sister, he began to sweep.

When the stable was clean, Damon asked if they could go for a walk. He wanted to see how much the neighbourhood had changed.

"Of course not," laughed Wynne. "We've got to sweep out the main attic yet."

Damon groaned. He didn't like the idea of going back inside the house, especially now he had seen it from the outside.

"Come on," said Wynne, heading for the front door. "The sooner we start, the sooner we can have some time for ourselves."

"So sensible," muttered Damon.

"Sorry?" Wynne glanced over her shoulder.

"Nothing," said Damon.

The Witch Mother seemed to have disappeared. Damon didn't see her as they passed through the hallway – which appeared to have grown during his short absence. He noticed that the bare stone walls were hung with grotesque paintings of women who resembled the Witch Mother, and men who looked just as ferocious. Their faces shimmered in the strange light that Damon realised was coming from three burning torches fixed at intervals around the walls. He glanced up. There was no electric light.

"Don't we have electricity here?" he asked Wynne.

"What?" Wynne glared at him, her concern deepening.

"Never mind," said Damon. "Where can I wash? My hands smell of horses."

"How about in one of the bathrooms," suggested Wynne.

"Where are the bathrooms?" asked Damon, in a mockery of Wynne's tone. He had already seen that there was no downstairs bathroom like at home. Where the bathroom door should have been was a great bookcase, that he couldn't recall seeing before. The books were covered in a thick layer of dust and cobwebs.

Wynne placed a small, grubby hand on either side of Damon's head and stared into his eyes.

"What are you doing?" demanded Damon.

"Trying to see if something's got inside you," said

Wynne, squinting as if to view an object on a distant horizon.

"What do you mean?"

"You're behaving a bit like you did when that poltergeist possessed you. I know mother said she'd exorcised it, but she's not always that efficient is she?"

Damon yanked his head free. "Get off me. I'm not possessed by anything."

Wynne shrugged and began climbing the stairs, sighing with each step. Damon followed. There seemed to be more stairs than before and the banister, he saw, was shaped like a snake. He touched it gingerly, but it was made of wood and was not about to bite him or squeeze the life from him. When they reached the small landing, Damon saw that rather than ending, as he was sure they had done when he had first set eyes on the Witch Mother, the stairs continued upwards to a second larger landing lit by a massive iron candelabra.

To the right of the small landing, opposite the Witch Mother's bedroom was a door. In the real world this door would have led to Damon's bedroom. He couldn't resist taking a peek to see if this had changed as much as everything else.

"Wait!" he barked at Wynne, and pushed the door open.

"Damon!" Wynne grabbed his shirt and pulled him backwards.

"What?" Damon flung her an intense stare and then looked through the doorway. He could see nothing but darkness, but it wasn't ordinary darkness, it was like staring into a room full of molasses or tar. Then the blackness began to shift, to stir like something living. Wynne pushed Damon to one side and slammed the door shut. "What are you playing at?" she demanded.

"Stop screeching at me!" shouted Damon. "What's in there that's so dangerous?"

"You know what's in there! Stop acting like this, it's not my fault mother's upset you."

"What's in there?" demanded Damon, gripping

Wynne's tiny wrist and twisting it until she screamed in pain.

"Stop it!" Wynne, punched his shoulder with her free hand and Damon released her, shocked at someone actually retaliating.

Wynne ran up the second flight of stairs. Damon heard her sob as she turned right and disappeared from view. Damon smiled. It felt good to be acting more like his old self again. Then he glanced at the room full of blackness and felt afraid – and lonely.

"Wynne!" he called, chasing after her. "Wynne, wait!"

Chapter Four

Damon found Wynne crying in a small, square bathroom. The walls of the room were painted bright orange in contrast to the greys and browns that dominated the rest of the house.

Wynne was sitting on the side of an iron bath, her face hidden behind a grey towel.

"Don't cry," he said, grumpily.

"Why are you being so horrible?" asked Wynne, her voice muffled by the towel.

"I'm just fed up with this place," said Damon. "And I don't like girls telling me what to do."

"I always tell you what to do. Usually you just do it."

"Do I?"

"You know you do."

"Well that's all going to change from now on. But I won't make you cry again, not today."

Wynne sniffed back the next downpour of tears and frowned. Damon frowned back at her. "Why is this room

33

painted so brightly?" he demanded.

"Because I painted it, didn't I," Wynne was looking at him like she was a doctor and he the patient.

"Doesn't she care?" asked Damon, referring to the Witch Mother.

"Why should she care what colour the bathrooms are?" replied Wynne. "She never washes."

"Doesn't she smell?" Damon pulled a face as if he had just bitten into an apple and found half a maggot.

"You know as well as I do that she does," said Wynne. "Now keep your voice down. She may not have left to go and see you know who yet."

"Who?"

"The Pink Witch." Now it was Wynne's turn to pull the maggot-in-the-apple face.

Damon didn't like the sound of the Pink Witch – the grey Witch Mother was unpleasant enough.

"Come on," said Wynne standing with a sigh and heading back onto the second landing. "We'd better get on and sweep out the attic. And when we've done that I think we should sit quietly somewhere and talk about what your problem is. I know boys are supposed to go through a bit of a funny patch at about your age, but this is all very sudden. I still haven't ruled out magic or possession."

The walk to the attic took them up several more flights of stairs that seemed to have materialised from nowhere, during the short time Damon had been speaking to Wynne in the bathroom. The higher they went the colder and greyer their surroundings became. The stairs, which had been carpeted – albeit in grey carpet – in the lower reaches of the house, were bare stone higher up, the cool walls closing in on the children as they climbed.

Finally they reached a tiny landing no bigger than a door-mat above which, set in the ceiling, was a trap door. Wynne took a long pole that leaned against the wall and poked the door open. It slammed back against the floor of the attic and a cloud of dust blew down, stinging their eyes and making them cough.

"How do we get up there?" asked Damon, between chokes, squinting up at the attic entrance.

"The same way we always get up there," said Wynne, now prodding inside the attic with the pole. "Got it!" As she pulled the pole down a length of thick rope dropped with it. It looked to Damon like the tail of a giant rat.

"I'm not climbing up that," he said, moodily.

"Like you have a choice!" Wynne was already shinning up into the attic like a lithe monkey.

While Damon didn't like the idea of climbing the rope, he refused to be out-shone by a girl and so, with far more difficulty and heavy puffing than his new sister, he climbed after her, eventually clambering into the attic with a red, damp face.

"At last," said Wynne, who stood holding a broom in each hand, looking down at him.

Damon crouched on the attic floor, which wasn't nearly as dusty as he had expected, trying to catch his breath. Wynne shook her head, letting one of the brooms clatter to the ground. With the other she began to sweep, her small face contorted with the effort.

"It's not even dirty," said Damon, glancing round at the vast, empty space. Above his head great wooden beams crisscrossed each other like railway lines on a map, disappearing into the darkness of the pointed roof.

"It has to be spotless before mother will perform magic though, doesn't it? It's the only time she ever worries about cleanliness. She doesn't want something dropping into a potion that shouldn't be there and ruining everything. Do you remember when that fly fell into her cauldron while she was trying to create a tonic to make her more beautiful?"

"No," said Damon, trying to feign a lack of interest, when in fact he was desperate to hear what had happened.

"You're starting to really worry me now, Damon. Just how much stuff have you forgotten since this morning? What were you doing while you were hiding. Did you eat, drink or read anything suspicious?"

"Shut up about that for a minute and tell me what

happened to your mother when the fly fell into her cauldron."

"She grew a great long tongue and kept vomiting on her food before she ate it – just like a fly," Wynne recalled with a smile. "I must admit, it was a relief when the Pink Witch came up with a potion to reverse the spell. It was the constant buzzing that really upset me."

"Disgusting," said Damon, standing and shaking his arms, which ached from the climb. He glanced around again and this time noticed a small window set in one of the sloping walls. "Great!" he exclaimed, running across the attic and crouching so that his face was level with the small pane of glass.

"What's great about it?" asked Wynne, growing increasingly perplexed at her brother's strange behaviour. "Are you planning to help me at all today?"

Damon ignored her; at last he had a chance to really see how much different this world was from his own. From the top of the Witch Mother's house he'd have a perfect view.

CHAPTER FIVE

It was an alien landscape that Damon saw through the window: a network of rough, earthy roads and hills topped by ancient churches, their spires pointing to the dark sky like clawed fingers. And dotted amongst all this rustic, archaic strangeness, the occasional set of semi-detached houses, almost like those he had left behind. He studied the nearest collection of homes more carefully, trying to decipher a difference between them and those of his world. They had the same orange-tiled roofs (or did they?); the same metal-framed windows (or perhaps not); cars parked in the front drives, just like in Ickrington (or was he mistaken?). As he stared, his vision blurred. He wiped his eyes with the sleeve of his jumper and looked again. There were no semi-detached houses, but odd-shaped cottages with thatched roofs and where he was sure he had just seen double-glazed windows he now saw stained glass and wooden frames, panes of glass sectioned by strips of lead. He had to squint to make these

39

features out, because he was at least a hundred feet from the ground, but as his vision cleared, he found he could see much better than he had ever seen before. And where he had seen cars just seconds earlier, he now found battered old carts, carriages and, in one muddy front garden, a wheelbarrow heaped with coal.

"Damon!" Wynne's irritated voice cut through his thoughts.

"What?" he turned, feeling dizzy and more confused than ever.

"Will you please help me!"

He felt too dazed to argue. He stumbled to the fallen broom and retrieved it from the floor, feeling his head swim as he bent over.

"Are you okay?" asked Wynne, placing a hand on his shoulder.

"Yes!" snapped Damon, and to stop her questioning him any further he began to sweep. All he ever seemed to do in this world was sweep.

When their chore was completed, Wynne gave a satisfied sigh and leaned her broom against the nearest wall. Damon followed suit and without even thinking about it he picked up the large metal dustpan into which they had swept the pile of dust collected from the floor.

"Thanks," said Wynne, relieved that her brother appeared to be returning to his old self. "Let's go and get something to eat and then we'd better hide in the stable in case the Pink Witch comes back with mother."

Damon shuddered at the mention of the Pink Witch.

"What's she like?" he asked.

"What do you mean?" Wynne was half way down the rope that lead from the attic.

Damon handed down the dustpan, before sitting with his feet dangling over the edge of the trap doorway.

""The Pink Witch. What's she like?"

"You know what she's like – she's hideous and incredibly evil."

Damon's mind was not set at ease by this

description.

2

They ate a light meal of cheese and bread, which Damon felt was far too light,

"I need some more food!" he insisted, glancing around the great, draughty kitchen. He jumped from the chair at the long, dark wooden table and began to search on the shelves that lined the stone walls.

"Lizard's eye!" he exclaimed, glaring at the label on one of the array of jars that filled the shelves. "Toad's foot!" His eyes scanned the first row of oddities. "Owl's claw, cat's whisker, gerbil's nose juice!"

Wynne shrugged. "So what?"

"I want peanut butter or jam, not mouse bogies!" Damon flung the jar against the nearest wall, grinning as it shattered and sparkling shards of glass scattered across the stone floor.

"Damon!" Wynne leapt to her feet.

"Don't say a word!" warned Damon. "If you nag me about one more thing I'll hit you – it wouldn't be the first time I'd hit a girl."

Wynne opened her mouth to protest, but Damon pressed two fingers to her lips and said very clearly and very close to her startled face: "Don't even think about it!"

Wynne stumbled backwards, eyes bulging.

"Now," said Damon. "Where's the fridge?"

Wynne looked blank.

"Where do you keep the food in this mad house?"

"Damon, stop it, you're not funny."

Damon was about to tell Wynne exactly what he thought of her but was interrupted by the sound of hooves clattering up the driveway to the house.

"Quick!" Wynne leapt up, running towards a door at the far end of the kitchen. "Hurry!"

Damon was torn between refusing to do what a girl told him to do and the thought of having to meet the Witch Mother again, or even worse, the Pink Witch.

Wynne had pulled open the door and a gust of fresh, chill air blew in from the back garden.

A strident cackle sounded from outside. It was a dreadful sound that made the contents of Damon's stomach churn. He no longer felt hungry.

"Come on, Damon!" whispered Wynne urgently. "We can't let the Pink Witch see us!"

Damon made his decision, running the length of the kitchen and leaping down the back steps.

"We have to get into the stable without her seeing us," said Wynne pushing the door closed.

"Why?" Damon was shivering. He told himself it was because of the cold and not the thought of the Pink Witch or the memory of her evil laugh.

"If she knew mother had children she'd probably kill her – and us."

"But why?" asked Damon, as Wynne tugged him towards the low gate that led to the driveway.

"Damon, have you forgotten everything?"

44

"Maybe," said Damon, crouching with Wynne by the gate.

"The Pink Witch is allergic to children. We bring her out in horrible welts or something. That's what mother says anyway."

Damon decided to remain hiding until he'd seen the Pink Witch for himself.

"Yuck!" Wynne nodded down the driveway, which appeared to have doubled in length since Damon had walked along it earlier that day. Through a gap between the slats of the gate he saw a grotesque, bizarrely shaped carriage, with oversized wheels like those from the pram of a giant baby. The vehicle looked like an exotic pink vegetable – bloated at either side, narrow at each end. A princely horse, its coat dyed pink and its mane plaited with pink ribbons, stood at the fore. A gaunt little man with black hair that clung to his long neck like seaweed sat astride the horse, a vicious leather whip hanging docile in his white, withered hand.

"I'll have Brackwell fix the wheel on your cart when

45

I come tomorrow," said a voice from the carriage. Like that cackling laugh that had sent them fleeing from the kitchen, the voice made Damon's hair pull at his scalp and his stomach lurch.

"Thank you Agnes." The Witch Mother, sounding unusually meek, climbed from the side of the carriage nearest to the gate. "Would you like to come in?" she asked glancing over her shoulder.

"No, no. I shall see you tomorrow when we can finalise our plans."

A pale, long-fingered hand, the nails painted lurid pink, reached out of the carriage, pulling the door closed. With a flick of the evil whip, the driver sent the horse galloping up the driveway.

"That was like something from a nightmare," whispered Damon, referring to the hideous carriage and its passenger.

"Every day is like a nightmare here," replied Wynne.

Chapter Six

"We'd better sneak into the house and get to bed," said Wynne when they had heard the front door close behind the Witch Mother. "She won't want to see us tonight. Her head will be full of whatever evil ritual they're planning now."

Damon just nodded. He felt exhausted. They crept back through the kitchen, and the room of books, which was now so big it felt to Damon like walking through a forest of dusty volumes, and into the hallway.

"Good night then," said Wynne, darting up the first flight of steps, which was no longer carpeted, but bare, chill stone.

"Don't we sleep in the same room?" asked Damon, suddenly terrified at having to sleep alone in this weird changing house.

"No we don't!" Wynne scowled.

"Where do I sleep then?"

"In your room."

"Which is where?"

But Wynne had disappeared into the gloom of the first landing. He heard her light footsteps continue upwards and gave chase.

The dark scared Damon. Even in the cosy semi that was his real home, shadows took on monstrous forms at night. Here there was the strong possibility that the shadows might really conceal monsters. Damon stopped on the first landing. He knew that the door to the right was not his bedroom – he remembered the churning blackness with a shiver. The room to the right had been the Witch Mother's bedroom that morning, but the way things shifted in this house, it could have changed. Damon decided not to risk looking and continued on to the next, much larger, landing. There was no sign of Wynne. He wandered from door to door, past the small bathroom where he had found Wynne crying earlier, past an open door that lead to a small room full of jars and the smell of disinfectant, and another that opened onto a room devoid of furniture where the floor was carpeted with dead flies. Damon hoped neither of these was his room. He wandered on along the corridor, both sides of which was lined with dark wooden doors.

"Go to bed!"

The thick, black voice came from the air around him. It was inhumanly slow and jarred Damon's insides with fear. He turned full circle, searching for a sign of the owner of the voice, but the corridor and the now distant landing were empty.

"Go to bed!" came the odious sound again and a banging began, like a huge fist hammering the wall, growing louder and louder. Damon screamed and ran. He fell against the wall at the end of the corridor and turned. The banging kept coming, so loud it hurt his head. He pushed open the nearest door and fell into the room beyond, slamming the door shut behind him. He stood in an icy cold bedroom, the bare stone walls flickering in the meagre light of a single burning torch.

The banging stopped and after a short silence the

slow, deep voice boomed, "Sleep well!"

Damon shuffled towards the large dusty bed. He didn't care whether this was his room or not, he needed to sleep. He said a quick, reluctant prayer, as he lay down, that he would wake in his own room, in his own world with his real mother there to make him breakfast.

He dreamed that night that he saw his mother looking down at him, crying and whispering his name. In the dream he reached out to touch her face. He wanted to say something nice to her, just in case he never got the chance again. But he woke to the sound of the Witch Mother shrieking his name.

"Damon! Get down here, you little brat!"

He wanted to cry as he climbed from the stale-smelling bedclothes and made his way to the stairs.

The Witch Mother, wearing the same ankle-length grey cardigan buttoned to her scrawny neck, slapped him across the head as he reached the hallway, now immense and filled with a swirling, noisy wind that made the portraits rattle against the walls.

"Is this house actually growing?" he asked, rubbing the sore place on his head where the Witch Mother kept hitting him.

She glared at him, eyes narrowing into slits of cold moonlight. "What?" she spat.

"It doesn't matter," said Damon.

Fortunately, Wynne appeared at the front door, which was now encased in a stone arch, defaced with the heads of grimacing gargoyles, and called to him with mock agitation. "Come on Damon, I'm not waiting all day!"

Damon followed her gratefully into the driveway, now more of a dirt track, with a high hedgerow that hid the neighbouring house from view – if it still existed.

"Does this place keep changing, or is it just me?" he asked. Wynne just gave him one of her puzzled looks and headed away from the house.

"I heard the monster last night," she said, as they reached a road just as muddy and only slightly wider than the driveway. "I wish mother would find a way of sending it

51

back to wherever it came from. I can't sleep once I've heard it crashing through the house. Did he show himself this time, or did you just hear him?"

"Have you seen it then?" asked Damon, disturbed at the prospect of the terrible voice having a body. "Where did it come from?" Damon, picked up a stick from the side of the road and began prodding at the savage looking hedgerow as they walked.

"Careful," said Wynne, "There may be birds nesting in there."

"That's why I'm doing it," said Damon. "Now answer my question. Where did the monster come from?"

"I don't know. It just appeared after one of her rituals, didn't it!"

"Is it dangerous?"

"Well it hasn't hurt us yet, has it?"

Damon took small comfort from this statement.

"Where are we going?" he asked.

"Anywhere, as long as we're not around when The

Pink Witch arrives. They're planning something really big. I think it might be happening tonight in the attic we swept out yesterday."

"A ritual?"

"What else?"

Damon detected the hint of a put-down in Wynne's reply. He was feeling upset and vulnerable today and, so to hide the fact, he gave Wynne a small shove.

"Damon!" she fell sideways, losing her arms in the scratching mass of hedgerow. "What was that for?" Her hand and lower arm were bleeding when she pulled them free.

"I just don't like your tone," said Damon. "You've got a small mouth with too much to say."

"I've got what?" Wynne looked flabbergasted.

"You heard. Stop talking to me like I was an idiot. You're the stupid one."

"Damon, what in Lightsleep has got into you?"

"What?"

"You really are possessed aren't you? Get out of my

53

brother!" Wynne screamed into Damon's face.

"Don't be ridiculous." Damon gave her another shove. "I'm just sick of being bossed around by a girl – especially a short, ugly little girl who's younger than I am."

Wynne shook her head and went to say something, but the sound of galloping hooves and the crack of a whip caught her in mid-breath. "The Pink Witch! She'll do something horrible to us if she sees us. Quick!" Wynne dropped onto the ground and crawled under the hedge. Damon hesitated for a second and then followed, complaining as thorns and sharp twigs raked at his face and arms. The sound of hooves grew closer. Damon peered out at the road and saw the hideous pink coach round the nearest corner. As it turned, the coach tipped sideways and a screeching voice called: "Careful you idiot. I nearly lost my wig!"

As the carriage passed where the children hid there was an air-splitting crack and one of the wheels spun away from its axle hitting the bank at the side of the road just inches from Damon's face. He heard the Pink Witch scream and his stomach coiled into a tight knot, like the first time he had heard her dreadful voice.

"What have you done, you idiot?"

The carriage door nearest to the children flew open and a long white leg emerged, the foot encased in a bright pink shoe, the toe so pointed it could have cut through ice, the heel long and dangerous like a dagger. From where he lay, trying not to breath too loudly, Damon could only see as high as the Pink Witch's knee, and this was soon covered by the hem of a lurid pink dress as she clambered onto the roadside.

"Don't just sit there, get down and fix it!" she screamed at the driver. "I'm a witch, not some tin-pot conjurer!"

Wynne's foot, which was almost touching Damon's nose, twitched nervously as the driver jumped down and crouched to retrieve the wheel, his gaunt, miserable face so close they could smell his rank breath. It smelt like old cabbage soup, left to stand in a hot kitchen for a week.

Damon wanted to close his eyes, but was scared that when he opened them the driver's face would be pressed close to his, putrid breath filling his nose until he choked on it.

Eventually, the dismal servant picked up the wheel and grappled it down the bank to the carriage, where the Pink Witch stood, still only a pair of high-heeled shoes and the hem of a dress to Damon. As the driver worked to fix the wheel back on she prodded him with her sharp shoes, barking orders and complaints. Finally, the wheel was in place and the Pink Witch climbed back into the carriage, still moaning, and the driver returned to his place with sad, lolloping steps. A loud crack of the whip and the carriage shot off, sending up a spray of mud and leaves, some of which spattered the children's faces, but they were too relieved to care.

Damon scrambled from beneath the hedgerow, groaning and whining at the state of his clothes and the pain of the cuts and scrapes he had endured.

"Oh shut up!" Wynne was red-faced, her small fists clenched at her side.

"What?" Damon turned on her, his own face trembling with anger. Nobody ever told him to shut up.

"You heard; you've been horrible lately. You're supposed to be my brother!"

"Yes, well, I'm not," said Damon through clenched teeth. "And if I was I'd get as far away from you as possible, which is what I'm going to do right now."

Damon stomped down the bank and up the road, splashing mud as he went.

"What do you mean?" demanded Wynne, running after him and grabbing him by the arm. "What do you mean you're not my brother?"

"I'm not!" Damon stopped and pushed her hand away. "I come from another world. I don't belong in Lightsleep, or whatever you call this place. I was brought here by a funny little man with a big round head and a clipboard. I don't know where your brother is, all I know is that I've somehow ended up in his puny body and that he must be a right wimp if he lets you talk to him like you thought you could talk to me."

"I knew it!" Wynne looked almost pleased at the news that Damon was an impostor from another world. "I knew the real Damon wouldn't be so horrible. Maybe, if you go back to wherever you come from, my Damon will reappear here."

Damon gave her a hateful stare. "If I knew how to get out of this place, do you really think I'd still be here? I think I know what's happening though. I think this is a dream, a horrible, over-long nightmare, and I'm sick of going along with it. If this is a dream, I'm going to start doing the sort of thing I normally do in dreams."

"Like what?" Wynne planted a hand on each hip and waited for his answer.

"Fly?" said Damon, looking skyward.

CHAPTER SEVEN

Damon always flew in his dreams, and although he knew that this was not strictly a dream, he still felt a dream feeling inside, the feeling that anything was possible. If monsters could bellow at him to go to bed and pink witches draw up in pink carriages, flying should be no problem.

Wynne was staring at him as she had stared at him several times since his arrival in the land of Lightsleep. Damon decided not to fly off and leave her after all. He realised that a much more effective way to teach her who was boss would be to fly with her high above the ground until she screamed to be put down. Damon grabbed her by the arm and leapt into the air.

And landed on the ground again – heavily.

"Damon!" Wynne pulled her arm free. "Grow up!"

"Shut up!" shouted Damon. "I can fly. Just give me time to make it work. Stop acting like a typical, stupid, nagging girl. Why do girls always try and make boys feel babyish. You're the one that's always crying like a baby."

Wynne turned and began marching along the road, swinging her arms in a defiant manner.

Damon ran after her, fuming. He'd taken a few steps when the ground suddenly felt strange and soft. He looked down and realised it wasn't ground at all, but air. he was hovering at least two feet off the ground. He was flying. Or nearly flying.

He tried to call to Wynne, who was still marching ahead of him, but his voice had turned high and weak. He flapped his hands wildly and began to rise. When he was around ten feet from the ground he began to kick his legs and move his arms as if swimming. He tipped forward with a gasp and began to move through the air after Wynne. He swam harder, the air like treacle, his progress slow. Finally, he was above Wynne and managed to call her name. She looked behind her, then confused she glanced upwards. She stared open-mouthed for a moment, then without speaking she reached out a quivering hand and Damon took it.

She felt light and Damon lifted her easily, taking her small frame under one arm and pushing through the air with the other until, after much effort, they had flown over the hedgerow and were making jerky progress across a vast field, beyond which lay the great forest that Damon had seen from the back garden of the Witch Mother's house.

"Flap your arm too," said Damon, his own limb aching from the effort of flying for both of them.

With Wynne's efforts they moved a little faster and rose a little higher, heading towards the outskirts of the forest. After much arm flapping and leg kicking they were reaching for the branches of a tree that stretched like the arms of a waiting parent into the field. They scrambled onto the thickest of the branches, swivelling round to sit with their tired legs dangling, sore and weightless. Damon couldn't remember flying ever being such hard work in any dream he'd ever had.

"Where...when did you learn to do that," gasped Wynne, her face flushed and wet with sweat.

"In my dreams," said Damon, 'which is what I was hoping this was."

"Well, I can tell you now, it's not," said Wynne, "because I've been here all my life, and I'm not part of your dream."

"Maybe, maybe not," said Damon, still catching his breath. "I can't think why I'd let someone as irritating as you into any dream of mine."

Wynne scowled. "Now what?" she asked looking down through the matrix of branches to the forest floor far below. Damon glanced down too and felt immediately sick. He snapped his head upright and gripped hold of the branch until his fingers turned white.

Wynne smiled. "The real Damon isn't afraid of heights."

"Nor am I." Damon's terrified face betrayed the truth.

"Why don't you just fly us both down," suggested Wynne.

"I don't think I can," said Damon, his eyed closed. "I think the power has gone. I don't feel it any more."

"Great," said Wynne.

2

It was about two hours later, when both children had completely numb bottoms and were sick of griping with each other, that a voice spoke to them from the uppermost branches of the tree. It was a high, musical voice, although tinged with suspicion and aggression.

"Are you trying to steal my eggs? If you are, you're going the right way to getting your eyes pecked out!"

The children looked up and gaped at the face that peered down at them. Two saucer-sized eyes were set on either side of a wide yellow beak. A wild array of white and red feathers formed the rest of the head and body of the bird, which was bigger than Damon.

"A parradowl." said Wynne.

"A what?" Damon looked from his otherworld sister

to the thing looking aggressively down at them.

"We're not after your eggs," Wynne assured the creature. "We're stuck. We didn't even know you were here. I didn't realise there were any parradowls left in Lightsleep."

"We're the last. Too many bad witches round here, that's why," replied the bird, losing some of the angry glint from its close-set eyes.

"You can say that again," mumbled Damon.

The parradowl cocked its head to one side and studied the children. "Tut, tut, tut," it said finally. "Fancy climbing up a tree if you don't know how to climb down."

"We didn't climb," said Damon. "We flew."

The creature's eyes widened. "That's a tall tale, young man," it squawked. "If you could fly up here, then you could fly down. Anyway little boys and girls can't fly, unless they're…you're not are you?" Suspicion and anger were suddenly replaced by fear in the bird's eyes.

"What?" asked Wynne.

"Witches," whispered the bird and its great fluffy

head turned full circle as if searching the area for further signs of their witchery.

"No!" blurted Damon.

"But our mother is," said Wynne, "and if we're not home soon she'll come looking for us. So would you mind helping us down?"

The parradowl puffed out its feathers so that it appeared to double in size. "I might,' it said finally. "But if I find out you've been lying and that you're just two nasty, egg-stealing children, I'll peck out your eyes. I will!"

Damon cringed, trying to remember what colour his eyes were so that he would be able to describe them to people when he was left with two scabby holes.

"They're not lying Toshi," came a higher-pitched voice from another tree. "I saw them while I was looking for food. They flew from the road over there, right across the field. Worst flying I've ever seen, mind you."

"I'm new at it," said Damon, turning to see a second parradowl flapping over to their tree, its wingspan wider than he was tall, its feathers completely white.

"I'll take your word for it, Heeshee, but I'm still uneasy about them. It wouldn't be the first time brats had stolen our eggs for the fun of it. Humans don't seem to realise that when they take our eggs they're killing our babies."

Damon remembered when he had taken the eggs from the nest of a blackbird and thrown them against a wall. He thought of the smell one of the eggs had left on his hands when he accidentally crushed it and wondered if it had been the smell of dead babies.

"Are you a couple then?" asked Wynne.

"Twenty-seven years," said Toshi, hopping down to their branch, and ruffling his feathers with pride.

"He's my lifelong mate," cooed Heeshee, lowering her eyes coyly.

"Yuck!" whispered Damon. Wynne jabbed him in the side with a sharp elbow. He scowled at her but didn't retaliate.

"I don't like that one," said Toshi, nodding towards Damon.

"Well then the sooner we get him out of our tree and away from my babies the better," said Heeshee, who was now perched on the opposite end of the branch from her husband, eying Damon menacingly.

"So you want to get down do you?" asked Toshi, amber eyes fixed on Damon.

"Yes," said Damon.

"Yes, please!" Toshi corrected him.

Damon hesitated. "Yes please," he said finally. Saying please felt almost as weird as saying sorry.

"I want to check one thing first," Toshi edged closer to Damon, who glanced warily at the bird's sharp beak. "Is your mother a good witch or a bad witch?"

"Oh, a good witch!" Wynne assured him. "The kind of witch that created your kind all those years ago."

"Don't get ideas above your station, dear," said Heeshee, cocking her head haughtily. "The witches that created our kind were special, not the rag-tag bunch of spell-spinners that masquerade as witches these days. There's not a decent one amongst them. If the witches that created parradowls could see what had happened to that school..." Heeshee flapped a wing pointing off into the depth of the forest.

"The Pentagram School?" asked Wynne.

"Yes, of course the Pentagram School – once a seat of learning for young witches and warlocks from across Lightsleep, now just a sad, dismal boarding school for orphans and children whose parents just don't want them. Can you imagine, Toshi, a parradowl ever neglecting their own children like that?"

Toshi shook his head, tutting so rapidly he sounded like a lawn sprinkler.

"The witches that created parradowls from the feathers of a beautiful she-owl and a proud he-parrott and gave us the powers of wisdom and speech were true lovers of magic," continued Heeshee. "They wanted to improve their world, not pollute it with evil spells for self-gain..."

"So can you get us down or not?" asked Damon.

But Heeshee continued: "And now the most evil witch I've ever come across, the grotesque and vulgar Pink Witch, is planning a ritual that could upset the balance of this world forever. And she's even roped in some other second-rate witch to help her."

"Why does she need this other witch?" asked Wynne nervously, aware that the second-rate witch Heeshee referred to was her mother.

"Because the ritual involves children," replied the parradowl, "and the Pink Witch can't touch children. And I tell you now, dearie, I wouldn't want to be one of the children used in this ritual, because if I know the Pink Witch, they won't be alive come the end of it."

CHAPTER EIGHT

"How do you know all this?" asked Wynne, still reeling from the shocking news that her mother was about to become a child killer.

"I know a lot of things, dearie," replied Heeshee, preening the ruff of feathers around her neck. "Come across all sorts of information when I'm out hunting. The Pink Witch's home – if that monstrosity can be called home – is set in the middle of my hunting ground. Lots of mice and rats scurrying all over the place. I take my life into my hands every time I go there, but we have to eat and that's where the food is…"

"Get to the point, dear," coaxed her husband.

Heeshee shot him a moody glance. "Getting to the point then," she continued. "I was perched in a tree just outside the window to one of her lewdly decorated rooms when I heard her talking to this other witch. She mentioned a spell and something to do with a magic talisman that could contain the essence of evil. I also heard her mention needing seven children and the Pentagram School. Well, this sparked my curiosity and although I know it didn't do the cat any good, I edged a little closer to the window and peeked in. There she was dressed in one of her hideous pink frocks, lying on a sofa – pink, of course – eating a massive bar of chocolate. The other witch, a drab little thing all in grey, was sitting cross-legged on the floor, looking up at the Pink One like she was a goddess. 'You'll have to get the children and conduct the ritual,' she was saying, between mouthfuls of chocolate, 'and you'll have to get them tonight and keep them until the following night when the ritual must be performed.' Well, they chatted on for hours and I was able to glean most of what is going on. The spell, as I understood it, will contact the spirit of a long-dead warlock who discovered the whereabouts of this powerful talisman, so powerful it could control pure evil and channel it to the owner's will. Imagine Toshi, being able to control pure evil and use it for your own horrible ends."

Toshi tutted.

"Well," continued Heeshee, "this Warlock – I think his name was something like Sebastian Barthwait or Barthwhistle – had already acquired a tiny piece of pure evil, which he kept in a magic jar, so he went in search of the talisman, leaving his seven children to fend for themselves – their mother had died given birth to the seventh. He found the talisman after months of searching, but when he returned triumphant to his home, all his children had died of hunger. Even though he was a wicked man, he was devastated. He took the talisman miles from his home and buried it in a secret place. He then took the jar containing the pure evil and buried that miles from the talisman. And then he killed himself and his spirit, apparently, went in search of the spirits of his dead children. Bit too late to start trying to be a caring father by then if you ask me, but…"

"And the spell?" prompted Wynne.

"The spell with the seven children is designed to fool his wandering spirit into thinking he has found his children and trap it in a magic circle until he reveals the hiding place of the talisman."

"And when she finds the talisman..." began Wynne.

"She'll use it to become the most powerful witch in the world and destroy anyone that gets in the way."

"Only if she has a piece of pure evil, dear," said Toshi.

"Oh, but she has," Heeshee bobbed up and down excitedly. "Or at least the other witch has. The Pink Witch, so I gather, makes her keep it in a room in her house. The room's protected by some spell, apparently, and the pure evil just keeps growing and growing, feeding off the evil vibes floating round the house. Without the talisman it's just a useless, nasty mass of blackness – that's what the Pink Witch says, but I think she's just saying that to stop the other witch complaining. I'm pretty sure that if the pure evil grows much more it could break out of the room and destroy everyone in that house and then...goodness only knows."

Damon glanced at Wynne, who had turned deathly

white. "That's what I saw, isn't it," he whispered.

Wynne tried to hush him, but Heeshee's keen hearing had picked up every word.

"You've seen the pure evil?" she asked. "Where?"

"In her house," said Damon. "Her mother's the witch that's helping the Pink Witch. This is nothing to do with me, I come from another world. I've somehow managed to swap places with her lame brother."

"I thought so," said Toshi. "Thought I felt a bit of a tremor yesterday morning? We said it'd be something like that, didn't we dear? Was it about eleven o'clock in the morning that you came over?"

"Probably," said Damon, amazed that the big bird knew about anything more than catching rats.

"We're very sensitive to that sort of thing," explained Heeshee, with pride. "Not much cross-world activity gets past us."

Their conversation was interrupted by the dull sound of hooves on wet ground and the creak of wooden wheels.

The four tree-dwellers turned towards the sound and saw, some way off into the forest, the stooped sorry figure of the Pink Witch's servant, pulling on the reins of Barrow, the horse Damon had fed the previous day. Barrow was pulling a large wooden box on wheels. Attached to the front of the box was a small seat, upon which perched the Witch Mother, wrapped in a limp black cloak.

"She's going to the Pentagram School to kidnap the seven children," whispered Wynne. "We have to stop her."

"Don't try and involve me in all this," said Damon. "This is nothing to do with me."

"Oh yes it is," said a voice in his head. "I still have the clipboard, remember." Damon recognised it as that of the funny little man who had brought him to this odd world. He sighed and in his grumpiest voice asked Wynne: "How exactly do you intend to stop her?"

"I don't know," said Wynne shaking her head in dismay. "What can I do? I'm just a kid, how can I stop two witches?"

"You're not on your own in all this," Heeshee reminded her. "Our kind don't want this ritual to take place any more than your lot do. Me and Toshi will help, won't we Toshi?"

"I suppose we'll have to," agreed Toshi, rounding the sentence off with a loud tut.

"Maybe, when this all comes to light, King Arold will get his act together and clamp down on witches and warlocks using their powers willy-nilly for all sorts of selfish reasons," said Heeshee. "He used to be such a fine man before he found out about Queen Arabella and that chef."

"Who's King Arold?" Damon asked Wynne, but Heeshee picked up on the question.

"Who's King Arold? You really are from another world aren't you. King Arold," she said slowly as if talking to an idiot, "is the ruler of Lightsleep. He was once a good king, who was quite skilled in the art of magic. Now King Arold's magic is all washed up in a bottle of wine and Queen Arabella is forever smiling and looking very well fed. Why the chef hasn't been executed by now, I don't know. Parradowls I've spoken to who've perched near the palace say he's so broken hearted he doesn't have the will to do anything to stop them carrying on."

"And how are we going to stop mother killing seven children and helping the Pink Witch take over the world?" asked Wynne politely.

"Yes, right," chirped Heeshee. "Can you still fly, boy?" she asked Damon.

"I don't think so." The flying feeling had completely left Damon. He knew that if he tried he would drop to the ground like a stone, the thought of which made him queasy.

"Then Toshi, you'll have to carry him to the Pink Witch's house. Find the book or manuscript, or whatever the spell is written on and destroy it. At least that might delay things a bit. I'll take the girl to the Pentagram school and try and warn the children."

"And who'll be looking after our unborn children while we're flying off all over the country trying to save the world?' asked Toshi, head cocked to one side, clawed foot tapping the branch.

"Oh my goodness!" gasped Heeshee. "How could I forget my babies? I feel like such a terrible mother. I just got so caught up in everything. Wait here." Heeshee launched herself from the branch and flew off, weaving through the trees with an agility not suggested by her size.

"She's all worked up now," sighed Toshi. "She won't rest until she's sorted this whole mess out – or until we're all dead."

CHAPTER NINE

Heeshee returned minutes later.

"I've found us a baby-sitter," she said, alighting on the branch. Her next sentence was drowned by the sound of beating wings. Damon saw a shadow the size and shape of a small plane skid along the forest floor. He shuddered and looked up to see a massive bat diving through the tree tops, its great leathery wings wrapping around its giant rat-like body.

"I hate bats," he hissed as close to Wynne's ear as possible.

"Keep your opinions to yourself then," advised Heeshee. "This is Blackwing," she nodded towards the six-foot bat that now hung upside-down from a branch just above their heads. "Blackwing's the only other talking non-human besides us Parradowls left in this part of Lightsleep."

"Pleased to meet you," said Wynne. Damon just stared.

"I'll just go and cover the eggs with moss and leaves to keep them warm," said Heeshee.

"I can always drape a wing over the nest if the temperature drops too low," said Blackwing as Heeshee flew up through the branches to her nest. "Strange business this."

"Yes," agreed Toshi. "It is. I'm just sorry she's got you involved. Could all be her imagination. She gets bored you see, hunting all day and half the night, but you know us Parradowls, if we don't eat properly..."

"You drop dead," said Blackwing.

"Yes," said Toshi with a small shudder. "How's your brood, Blackwing?"

"Not bad, Toshi, not bad. They miss their mother, and not one of them talks human yet."

"Shame," said Toshi.

"Can't be helped. It's the atmosphere I think. Too much bad magic floating around."

Heeshee brought the conversation to an abrupt halt, swooping back onto the branch and launching into a list of commands. "Come along," she finally ordered Wynne. "Let's get going. We need to beat your mother to the school by at least a couple of hours if we're to stand any chance of getting those children to safety. Toshi, you be careful, don't try and be a hero. Just destroy anything with that spell written on it. Come and join us at the school when you're finished. If we're not there we'll be hiding somewhere in the woods."

"Yes, dear." Toshi jumped miserably from the branch, hovering in front of Damon. "If I'm not back by morning assume I'm dead."

Toshi rose a little and reached out both powerful talons hooking them through the shoulders of Damon's jumper.

"Hey!" Damon began to protest, but Toshi had lifted him from the branch and shot off across the field before he could utter another word.

Damon screwed his eyes shut and gripped hold of Toshi's dangling legs.

"Wait!" he shouted. "Before we go to the Pink

Witch's house, shouldn't we go to the house where the ritual is going to happen?" He opened his eyes a crack, saw grass whizz past below and shut them again. "I mean, if that's where the Witch Mother is actually doing the ritual, she'll have a copy of the spell there, won't she?" It was difficult to talk with wind pouring into his mouth, but he persevered. "There's no point destroying the Pink Witch's copy if there's still one at the Witch Mother's house, is there!"

"Gosh!" exclaimed Toshi flying round in an arc and hovering. "You're right. Didn't have you down as intelligent. Blimey, you have taken me by surprise. Where does the girl's mother live then?"

Damon opened one eye and scanned the countryside. Apart from a few thatched cottages, the Witch Mother's house was the only dwelling in sight. He pointed across the miles of farmland they had covered during the short flight. "There. The one with the towers and the bats."

"Right," said Toshi, propelling himself in that direction.

Damon, who had decided to be helpful until he could think of a way of getting home and out of this hideous situation, kept his mouth and eyes shut until he felt something solid beneath his feet. They were on the roof of the Witch Mother's house, amidst a cluster of ramshackle chimney pots, all black with soot. Toshi was perched on top of one scanning the roof for a way inside.

"There's a skylight leading into the attic where the ritual's going to take place," said Damon. "Unless that's gone now. Nothing about this place or this house seems to stay the same for long."

As Damon crawled across the sloping roof, he wondered if the secret to getting back to his own world lay somewhere inside the house. Maybe the doorway between the worlds was inside the room of pipes.

"And how exactly are you going to find it?" asked the funny little man, inside Damon's head. "As you just pointed out, this place has a habit of changing."

"Shut up!" hissed Damon, spotting the sky-light and

scrambling towards it.

"It's open a crack," he said, sliding his fingers inside and releasing the catch. He swung his legs over the now open window, lowering himself to the newly swept floor. Toshi squeezed in behind him and flew up onto one of the wooden beams.

A large circle had been drawn on the floor, inside of which was painted a red seven-pointed star. A small section of the circle had not been drawn, perhaps to allow the Witch Mother a way in before she began the ritual.

"Find the spell and let's get out," hissed Toshi, hopping nervously from one foot to the other. "There's a small chest over there. Maybe that's where she keeps it."

The small wooden chest was sitting at the edge of the attic entrance. It had not been there the previous day when he and Wynne had swept. Damon crouched down to open it and as he did so he noticed the attic hatch was open and that a strange man was staring up at him. Damon froze with his hand on the catch of the chest, staring at the odd stranger. He was tall and thin, his hair yellow, lank and wet looking, his eyes dark, the lids heavy, making him look tired. He had a prominent nose shaped like an old-fashioned clothes peg with a spherical blob on the end. He was dressed all in black, reminding Damon of a funeral director he had once seen leading a procession of cars.

"Who are you?" the man asked, and Damon recognised the voice of the invisible demon from the previous night. It sounded like it was coming from underground, full of earth and grime. It was a rotten sound, a dead sound. As Damon stared, the memory of the voice still chilling his insides, the man's face began to change, the nose growing longer still, the droopy eyes wider, the wet mouth slacker. Green slime began to ooze from the gaping nostrils. The mouth kept dropping and dropping, the skin around it stretching like warm clay, until the bottom lip hung below the man's chest. "You're not the son are you," the voice rattled. "I see what she misses."

Now the man's arms were growing, tendril-like

fingers reaching up through the attic entrance, groping for Damon's feet.

"Grab the box!" Toshi swooped down from the beam scooping Damon into the air. Damon cried with pain as the bird's talons sunk into his skin, but he managed to keep hold of the small chest as Toshi dragged him towards the window. Damon looked back and saw the gaping face, still oozing slime emerge into the attic, the elastic arms slithering towards him, hands slapping the floor like dying flat fish.

Toshi had forced himself through the skylight and was flapping his wings wildly. "Why isn't he flying away?" wondered Damon, who had fallen into a trance-like state. Then he realised that his trousers had caught on the latch of the window and that Toshi was unable to pull free. He heard the slap, slap, slap of the creature's hands, the slow, dead thud of his footsteps and suddenly broke free of the stupor, yanking the hem of his trousers from the rusting latch and calling to Toshi. "Fly! Quickly, fly!"

Toshi took off pulling Damon through the window

into welcome fresh air. He felt cold rubbery hands clutching at his feet, but Toshi was too fast and soon they were circling high above the house and for once Damon was glad to look down, just to see that the nightmare man was not still stretching upwards.

"Better get to the Pink Witch's house," said Toshi. Not sure we'll find it so easy to steal a spell from there."

CHAPTER TEN

1

Wynne found the flight to the Pentagram school exhilarating. She kept her eyes open for most of the journey when the brisk wind didn't force her to close them. They flew way above the trees, Heeshee carrying Wynne by her coat. It was midday by the time they caught their first glimpse of the school amidst the thick growth of the forest, a mass of dark, gloomy stone towers and spires protruding like a nasty wart from the side of a steep hill.

Heeshee dropped to within a few feet of the forest floor, a short distance from the school, and released Wynne, who landed nimbly on her feet.

"It'll take your mother hours to get here by horse," said Heeshee. "She's obviously not a very powerful witch."

"She didn't used to be a witch at all," said Wynne sadly. "Not a practising one anyway. She turned very strange when my father left us and then the Pink Witch arrived and totally warped her."

"Do you think she has her under some kind of spell?" asked Heeshee, hovering just in front of Wynne's face, her wide eyes full of curiosity.

"Possibly," said Wynne. "She uses her to do everything she can't or doesn't want to do. Like this ritual."

"Right," said Heeshee, as if suddenly remembering their reason for being here. "We need to find a way into the school without being seen by the headmistress."

"Is she a witch?"

"Oh yes," said Heeshee. "A particularly nasty one apparently, although not all that powerful. Her name is Ariadne – sometimes referred to as Ariadne the Awful."

"How did she become headmistress?"

"I think she started as a teacher years ago when it still had something of a reputation for producing skilled witches. Then when she took over as head – it's rumoured she fixed the election ritual somehow – that all changed. She got rid of all the talented witches and turned the school into the sorry place it is now. I doubt if any witchcraft has been taught here for years."

"Will the school be protected by witchcraft?" asked Wynne, bending to tie a shoelace that she had noticed trailing behind her during the flight.

"I would think so, dear. Although I would imagine most of the magic is there to stop people getting out rather than getting in. Your mother is probably the first person who actually wanted to get into the Pentagram school for half a century. Anyway enough gossiping, let's come up with some sort of plan."

Heeshee alighted on the forest floor and began waddling round Wynne in a tight circle, chirping to herself.

Wynne peered through the trees at the Pentagram School. She imagined being an orphaned child, dropped off in front of the grotesque building, making the walk up the steep driveway and the flight of stone steps to the great front doors. She shivered and for once felt grateful she lived at home with the Witch Mother.

"Wait here," said Heeshee, taking off and soaring up towards the school. Wynne sat with her back to a tree and pondered events of the past two days. She thought of her real brother, lost somewhere, maybe in the horrible Damon's world. She felt tearful but refused to cry. She'd shed enough tears recently.

Heeshee returned in a flurry of white feathers, landing daintily on the ground and resuming her waddling walk, this time around the tree against which Wynne sat.

"I think the best plan would be for you to get in as an orphan and warn the other children. I need you to get them all into the western-most tower. There's a window at the very top that doesn't seem to be protected by magic – our magical roots make us parradowls sensitive to that sort of thing. Ariadne the Awful probably thought it was too high up to bother with. Aim to get there within the next two hours, by which time I will have thought of a way of getting everyone out."

"Are you sure about this?" asked Wynne.

"Yes, yes!" insisted Heeshee.

"And what if she doesn't let me in?"

"I've never heard of any child being turned away. They're not exactly queuing up for places there."

Wynne stared up at the ominous doors. Soon she would no longer have to wonder what it felt like to climb up to them and wait for Ariadne the Awful or one of her minions to usher her into the gloomy depths of the school.

"Well, go on," insisted Heeshee, fluttering her wings. "I'll see you and all the other children in two hours in the western tower. I'll get you all out and then we'll make a run for it and find a safe place to hide further into the forest."

Wynne climbed to her feet, feeling as sick as Damon had felt when he'd looked down from the tree.

"I'll see you in two hours then," she said, taking a few cautious steps. "If you're sure this is the best way."

But Heeshee was waddling in a circle again and chirping. Wynne took a deep breath and started out for the Pentagram School.

2

Damon and Toshi had been perched in a tree overlooking the Pink Witch's house for more than an hour. The house was as gruesome as Damon had expected – bigger than the Witch Mother's and exhibiting bad taste in every pink dome and turret.

Damon moaned for the umpteenth time about the cold, tugging the sleeves of his tatty jumper over his chapped hands; Toshi tutted for at least the thousandth time and they both stared miserably at the Pink Witch's carriage which was parked in the winding driveway to the house, the poor pink-dyed horse still tethered to it.

"If you hadn't made such a fuss about flying we might have beaten her back from your house," said Toshi between tuts.

"It's not my house, and I couldn't help feeling sick." Damon folded his arms and pouted angrily. "You go in and find the spell book on your own if you're such a hero.

Believe me, I couldn't care less if the Pink Witch and the Witch Mother sacrifice a bunch of brats. All I care about is getting home."

"Well, she doesn't appear to be planning to go out again," said Toshi, ignoring Damon's sulk. "So we may as well risk going in now. We'll probably die whether she 's there or not, so what the heck!"

Damon pulled an exasperated expression, then returned to sulking.

"Come on then," Toshi fluttered off of the branch and hooked his claws through Damon's jumper. "Ready?"

Damon sighed. "I suppose so. The man with the melon-head better show up after this, or I'll start casting a few evil spells myself."

"I wouldn't be surprised if you could," said Toshi, hoisting Damon out of the tree and flying over to the nearest open window. "Just pray it's not protected by magic," he said, glumly. "Or we'll both be fried."

Damon opened his mouth to protest, but Toshi had

already flown into the room beyond. Damon closed his eyes and tensed against the prospect of being cooked. But the Pink Witch was too confident of the protection offered by people's fear to bother with magically protected windows. Damon opened his eyes to find himself standing in a vast room the walls of which were painted lurid pink. He imagined all the rooms here would be painted the same colour.

There was little else of note about the room except the gaudiness of the furniture – pink sofas and chairs with gold fringes dropping to the pink carpet, golden candelabras holding pink candles and a life-size statue of a gargoyle standing in one corner, glaring menacingly at the new arrivals.

Toshi turned his head 360 degrees and tutted. "No books in here."

Damon walked to the nearest door, resting his hand on the gold handle. He wasn't feeling brave, he just wanted to find the spell and get out of the house as quickly as possible.

"I wouldn't go through there if I were you," said a cold, deep voice. Damon turned to look back into the room. Toshi's head was spinning as he searched for the owner of the voice. Why did voices in this place never have an owner, though Damon, irritably. But this one did and Damon realised with a dreadful plunging feeling in his stomach who the owner was. The gargoyle statue was walking across the pink carpet with long creaking strides, its stone wings spreading behind it, flapping in terrible slow motion, its twisted mouth dropping open to reveal fangs of jagged rock.

CHAPTER ELEVEN

1

Damon pulled frantically at the handle, but the door was locked from the other side.

"Help!" he screamed at Toshi who was flapping around the room, sending up clouds of feathers. "Stop acting like a headless chicken and do something! You got us into this!"

The gargoyle took another stiff-legged stride towards Damon. "Can't get out there," it said, jaw creaking like its limbs. It reached out a cold hard hand, the talons scraping the air just in front of Damon's face. Damon leapt across the room, diving behind one of the numerous sofas. He was trembling so hard he could barely move. He wanted Toshi to take control again, grab him by the shoulders and fly them out of this hellish house. He realised, staring at his hands flat against the odious carpet, that he had left the small chest from the Witch Mother's attic on the branch outside the window.

Creak! Creak! Creak!

The winged shadow of the gargoyle fell across him –
bigger and even more terrifying than the monster itself.

"Get us out of here!" he shouted at Toshi, who he
could hear still squawking and clucking like a farm animal.
He crawled across the floor, heavy footsteps close behind and
the Creak! Creak! Creak! of each robotic stride.

"Do something you stupid bird!"

He reached a pink wall and stood, turning to face the
approaching monster. It was coming for him, slow but solid
and unstoppable, lethal talons reaching for his throat. Damon
searched the wall for a potential weapon. An iron bracket
holding a burning torch was set just above his right shoulder,
he reached for it, hoping it would be loose and come away
easily, imagined himself burying it in the head of his
attacker, chipping away at the demonic face. But instead, as
he grasped hold of the bracket with both hands, it pulled
down like a lever and Damon found himself falling through a

newly opened doorway. "Toshi!" he yelped, toppling into blackness. He heard a scrape and a thud as the secret door slid shut again and then silence.

2

The driveway up to the Pentagram school was lined with dead trees, their bare branches laced with cobwebs. The grass was brown and trampled into the dry earth. Wynne looked up towards the austere front doors and her heart plummeted. She placed a foot on the first stone step and took a deep breath before climbing up the second and third, another short pause for courage and she mounted the final two steps and stood staring at a frayed bell rope. "Just pull it," she whispered. "There can't be much in here you haven't seen before."

She took hold of the rope, which felt dirty and clammy, and without giving herself further time to think, she pulled. She had expected a deafening, gloomy chime, but instead the house filled with a jolly melody, like the tune to a nursery rhyme. Wynne thought she might even recognise it from the time before her mother had turned evil. Footsteps sounded from behind the door. Wynne realised the person approaching was skipping, and it was somebody bigger than a child. The doors were suddenly flung open and Wynne took a step backwards. Framed in the doorway was a woman of around sixty, her unnaturally blonde hair tied in bunches with yellow ribbons, her cheeks painted with red circles, her smile inane and impossibly bright. She was wearing a short lacy white dress and matching sandals and in her left hand she held the biggest lollipop Wynne had ever seen. "Hi! Hi! Hi!" she shrieked joyfully, yanking Wynne into the school.

The entrance hall was dazzlingly bright, lit by extravagant chandeliers holding hundreds of candles. The expansive floor was paved in white tiles and the walls and ceiling were decorated with an array of grinning, skipping and dancing characters – fairies, elves, toy soldiers, jovial fat giants and beautiful princesses in flowing gowns and glittering tiaras. Wynne stared around her, amazed by the total contrast of the bright happy interior and the grim exterior.

"Come and play," pleaded the woman excitedly, skipping towards an open doorway, from which an even brighter light shone. Wynne followed, trying to form a sentence to explain her visit, but Ariadne seemed perfectly happy to welcome her into the school without question.

The door led into an enormous room lit by more elaborate chandeliers and by natural light that streamed through a row of arched windows decked in white lace curtains that blew gently into the room like playful spirits.

The floor was covered in toys of every imaginable size and description – dolls, teddy bears, scooters and tricycles, hobby horses, rocking horses, farmyards and zoos, painting kits, building bricks and modelling clay. Weaving through the mass of playthings were children, around thirty Wynne estimated, some of them riding, others running and squealing, some stumbling along in apparent disbelief at the number of choices they had.

A small girl, her dark hair tied in bunches similar to

Ariadne's, rode close by where Wynne stood, her chubby, pale legs straining with the effort of pushing the pedals of her tricycle, as if she had been riding for hours. Indeed, her flushed, damp face suggested that she was long overdue a rest.

"That's it my sweetie-pie," encouraged Ariadne, giving the tricycle a gentle shove with her foot. "Keep playing. It makes me so happy to see you play."

And then Wynne saw the same strained look on the face of every child. Two boys playing catch looked exhausted, the armpits of their short-sleeved shirts stained with sweat, their bandy legs buckling beneath them at regular intervals; a group of children acting out a war game with beautifully painted tin soldiers were pushing the figures around with slow, tired movements, their eyes betraying desperation for sleep.

Ariadne, her over-painted face radiant, clapped her hands and grinned at Wynne: "What are you going to play, sweetie-pie?" she asked. "Oh, it will make me so happy to see you play."

Wynne perused the toys again, her eyes settling on a small blue scooter. "I'd like to play with that please," she said, walking towards it.

"Oh, yes that would be lovely," enthused Ariadne, clapping her hands again and having a celebratory lick of her massive lolly.

Wynne placed one foot on the scooter and kicked off, cringing at Ariadne's shrieks of joy. The scooter would give her a chance to cover the entire playroom in as short a time as possible, enabling her to check for doors that might lead to the west tower and, once Ariadne's excited gaze had left her, to warn the children of the need for escape. Ariadne the Awful, she decided, was not the terrifying spectacle she had been led to believe – just a sad woman who wanted to stay young. She considered telling Ariadne of the Witch Mother's impending arrival and plans to kidnap seven of her children, but instinctively she decided against this. Later she was glad of the trust she had placed in her instincts, because Ariadne was about to show why she had a reputation for being truly awful.

CHAPTER TWELVE

1

Damon hated the dark – the uncertainty over what his outstretched fingers might touch as he stumbled along the secret passage. He had no idea where he was going, or what was sharing the blackness with him. He could feel the rough stone of a wall to his right and cool, dusty air to his left, ahead and behind. He was scared to speak in case his voice woke something evil that would uncurl from its tortured sleep and crawl after him on its starved belly.

"Follow us."

Damon felt his insides chill at the sound of the whispering voice. It sounded like that of a small boy, just ahead of him, but invisible in the darkness.

"Come on, don't be frightened." This was a girl's voice, and like the boy she sounded gentle and kind, not evil or threatening in any way.

"Who are you?" asked Damon, as his heartbeat

began to slow. "I don't like taking orders from kids I can't even see."

"My name's Arthur," replied the boy.

"And I'm Catherine," said the girl, and Damon felt a light touch on his hand. "Come on," said Catherine, tugging gently at his fingers.

"I don't hold hands with girls," snapped Damon, pulling free. "I need to find a spell. Unless you're about to make yourselves useful I suggest you leave me alone."

The last thing Damon wanted was to be alone in this dark, narrow space, but he couldn't admit that.

"We know," said Arthur. "We'll show you where the book is with the spell written in it, but I don't think destroying it will make that much difference. It's in her head now, it might as well be written on her brain."

"Really?" Damon surprised himself with his disappointment. What did he care if the ritual took place? He was only doing this because he thought it would get him home and in front of the TV in time for the wrestling. "Is the

Pink Witch still in the house?"

"She is," replied the girl," but she's asleep, gathering her strength for when the time comes for her to storm the Royal Palace."

"I wouldn't want to bump into her," said Damon.

His guides were silent, which was more disturbing than if they'd simply agreed with him.

"There's another secret door just here," whispered Arthur, pushing him gently towards the wall. "Just above your head and to your right. Don't be afraid."

Damon groped for some kind of lever to release the door, but there was nothing like the bracket that had opened the entrance into the secret passage.

"Can you feel a loose brick?" came Catherine's calming voice. "Just find the loose brick and push it."

"I can't find it," insisted Damon, but then his fingers touched upon a brick that was slightly indented and he gave it a light shove. With a creak and a hiss a panel slid to one side, casting light into the passage and revealing a small room full of ancient-looking books.

Damon turned to see his guides but the passage was empty. He shrugged and stepped into the room. There must have been a hundred books, scattered across the floor – great dusty books, their pages yellow with age, small books that could fit into the inside pocket of a jacket, books with colourfully illustrated covers, books with ominously plain black covers and books with no covers at all, just frayed, crumbling spines. "The one you want is over by the fireplace," said Arthur, as the secret door began to slide shut. Damon spun round, but through the narrowing opening he could see no-one. And yet he still heard both children whisper: "Goodbye, Damon. Good luck!"

There were several smaller books piled next to the fireplace, which was large enough for someone of Damon's height to stand in. No fire burnt in the grate, but the charred remains of two thick logs, still smouldering, suggesting that the Pink Witch had recently sat on the fat pink chair that stood in the shadow of the towering mantelpiece and read the content of the spell that would bring her great power. Damon shuddered as he knelt by the unstable pillar of books. He picked up the small volume that crowned the column. The book had a dusty brown cover with a title written in gold lettering that had been worn illegible. On the first page the title was written again in a strange language, the words were long, the lettering black and spidery.

"Is this the one?" he asked himself, flicking through the musty-smelling pages. How could he tell? Then he came across a picture somewhere towards the middle of the book. In fact it was more a diagram than a picture, showing a seven-pointed star surrounded by an incomplete circle, exactly like the drawing on the floor of the Witch Mother's attic. Damon grinned and slipped the book into the waistband of his trousers. Footsteps sounded in the corridor beyond the room, clattering, tottering footsteps of someone wearing high-heeled shoes. Damon felt instantly sick. He ran to the section of wall through which he had stepped, but on this side the brickwork was covered by more pink wall-paper and despite his frantic prodding there was no way of distinguishing the single loose brick. He searched the room for a hiding place as the footsteps stopped outside the door. He felt the contents of his stomach curdle as the door handle was turned.

"Madam, would you like me to serve your tea in this room?" came a female voice, heavy with age and subservience. The door handle sprang back to its original position. Damon bounded towards the fireplace, realising with beating heart and pulsating head that this interruption would be his only chance of escape. He ducked beneath the mantelpiece and stood with the upper part of his body hidden inside the chimney. His lower half stood in the smoldering ashes of the hearth, smoke billowing around his leather boots.

"No. Lay the table in the dining room. Fill it with everything scrumptious in the kitchen. Plenty of chocolate!" came the Pink Witch's reply. "Place my favourite looking glass on the table so that I can admire myself while I'm eating and make sure the plates are clean. I don't want to have to kill another member of the serving staff for leaving nasty stains on the crockery."

And again the door handle was turned. Damon looked upwards. There were small metal rungs embedded in the side of the chimney. Even in his state of panic he wondered at his luck and began to climb, his feet just disappearing from view as the Pink Witch entered the room. He couldn't see her, of course, but he heard the door creak open and the clatter, tap, clatter, tap of her shoes. He stopped climbing, afraid that his efforts might be heard in the room below. His breathing sounded so loud in the confines of the chimney he was sure the Pink Witch's head would soon appear below him, her white, taloned hand reaching up to grasp his vulnerable feet.

For a moment there was no disturbance below, then a piercing cry cracked the silence. "Where is it? Where is my spell book? Someone has been in here and taken my book!"

Damon felt woozy with fear. He was torn between

remaining completely still and climbing with every last ounce of energy to the top of the chimney and away from the evil woman who was close enough to touch him.

"Climb!" came an urgent whisper close to his ear. "She'll smell you. You have to get out now!"

It was Catherine's voice and still there was no sign of her. Damon decided to put his trust in the invisible girl and began a frenzied ascent, feet slipping, hands so damp with sweat each rung seemed elusive.

"Who's that?" He heard the Pink Witch crawling into the fireplace, dared a quick glance downwards, saw a mass of pink hair emerge into the chimney.

"Hurry!" came the joint whispers of Catherine and Arthur. "Before she has a chance to conjure any evil magic. She'll kill you without a second thought."

Damon found he couldn't breathe. He tried to gulp in a mouthful of air, but his chest wouldn't rise and his throat had closed up very small.

"Hurry!"

The Pink witch was scrambling to her feet, any second she would look up and see him.

Damon climbed on, his arms aching, his head throbbing. He needed to breathe.

"Who's there? A child! Oh disgusting, it's a child and it has my book!"

The Pink Witch had seen him.

She began to chant in a low, angry voice. Damon heard a crackling sound and felt intense heat rising from below. He chanced another quick glance downwards and saw fire, raging, spitting fire rising towards him. But it wasn't normal fire – the type that grows and destroys indiscriminately – this fire was after Damon and Damon specifically. From the leaping flames a shape was forming, an almost human form, its head a blazing yellow, its arms flickering red, reaching upwards towards the stunned Damon. The leering, hateful face fixed its glowering eyes upon his and the fire demon rose faster.

Small hands pulled at Damon's clothes, urging him

onwards. The fire demon was just feet away. He could feel the soles of his shoes begin to melt.

Suddenly the chimney took a sharp turn and he was crawling rather than climbing. But the fire demon was following, flames licking at his heels, threatening to creep up his hot white legs.

He scrambled onwards like a frightened animal, sweat pouring down his face and back.

"Kill it!" he heard the Pink Witch shriek, and fire began to crawl up his ankles, disintegrating his socks. Damon screamed as the melting fibre scorched his skin. The chimney turned upwards again and Damon saw light. His lungs fit to burst, he leapt gripping the edges of the chimney, pulling himself over the top. He fell with a desperate gasp onto the pink slate roof, rolling down towards the guttering without a thought for his life, too relieved that if he did die, it wouldn't be from having the flesh burned from his bones.

A cool gust of air ruffled his hair. He heard a familiar tutting sound and felt claws slipping through the wool of his jumper and soon he was air-borne.

CHAPTER THIRTEEN

Wynne weaved the scooter among the playing children and scattered toys, trying to decide which child to confide in first. She surveyed their tired faces, the dark shadows beneath their dull eyes, the weary slump of their shoulders and the languid motion of their limbs. She spotted a boy sitting in a corner slightly separate from the other children, a curtain billowing around him, sometimes hiding his face and dark curly hair from view. He seemed intent on his play, which involved moving several colourful toy animals around a wooden farm. Although his face and posture betrayed fatigue, he appeared less despondent than his fellow players. Wynne guessed he was around twelve years old, making him one of the older children in the room. She pushed the scooter over to where he sat cross-legged on the floor, a toy cow gripped in one hand, a farmer, with one arm missing in the other. The farmer appeared to be leading the cow to a wooden shed, although the cow, acting under the influence of the boy, was keen to remain amongst the faded green painted grass of her field.

Wynne brought the scooter to a halt at his side and bent to whisper in the boy's ear. He glanced up, startled, his mouth frozen in a small circle, as if waiting for a friend to throw a peanut to him.

"I need to warn..." began Wynne.

"Don't!" hissed the boy, his hands still acting out the farmyard dispute while he stared at her.

"But it's important..." continued Wynne. A bolt of lightning shot down from the ceiling, sending children leaping and screaming in all directions, toys were blasted into pieces, doll's limbs mingled with the heads of tin soldiers and tangled bike wheels. Darkness descended on the room.

"You stopped playing," she heard the boy whisper, miserably.

A second bolt of lightning cut through the gloom and a bony hand grabbed Wynne by the shoulder and swung her round. Stifling a scream Wynne faced Ariadne, who now looked truly awful. Her powder-caked face was distorted

117

with rage, the painted mouth twisted, her eyes blazing with incredulous fury, her hair crackling and hissing with electricity.

"How dare you," she spat into Wynne's face. "How dare you!"

"But I..."

"Shut up!" Ariadne stamped her foot and more sparks crackled in the air around her.

"Don't you know how unhappy I become when children stop playing?" she asked, her fingers digging painfully into Wynne's shoulder. "It drains me." Ariadne, slumped, hanging her head and allowing the hand that held the lollipop to dangle like a lifeless animal in a butcher's shop window. "It makes me so tired and miserable." Here Ariadne pouted and held up the lollipop which glowed and released another bolt of lightning that bounced off the ceiling like the previous blasts, sending the children fleeing to every corner of the room.

"Sorry," ventured Wynne. "I didn't realise."

"Didn't realise!" Ariadne fell against the nearest wall, glaring at Wynne with gaping mouth and wide eyes, as if she had just revealed some incredible secret. "Didn't realise!" she repeated shrilly. Wynne cringed, preparing for a further lightning bolt, but Ariadne stood up straight, shaking her head and re-applying her grip to Wynne's shoulder.

"Listen, sweetie-pie," she said with forced tenderness, her ravaged face just inches from Wynne's. (Wynne saw that she had little yellow balls of gunge in the corner of both eyes.) "You don't stop playing until I say you can stop playing. You don't sleep until I say you can sleep and you get up and start playing again when I say you can get up and start playing again!" Ariadne took a deep breath and blasted out the final part of her speech: "Welcome to my home!"

Swaying slightly from her exertions, Ariadne licked her lollipop and light returned to the room, another lick and in a flash the broken toys had returned to their former splendour, a third and she seemed restored to her playful self.

"Now play!" she cried, clapping her hands and skipping off, as if nothing untoward had happened. Immediately all the children resumed their games, if anything, slightly refreshed following Ariadne's outburst. Wynne let out a relieved sigh and kicked off, once again weaving through the groups of children, desperately trying to think of a way of getting them all to safety. And suddenly it came to her, the most obvious plan she had ever formed.

She circled the room, her legs already feeling tired, until she again came within a few feet of the boy playing with the farm. As she passed him she called in a shrill whisper: "Run after me!" He looked up with the same startled expression that had previously greeted her. She beckoned agitatedly for him to follow her. He hesitated, the cow and farmer still gripped in each hand. Wynne pushed onwards, not daring to solicit another tantrum from Ariadne, who was happily skipping around the room, inspecting her occupied minions. Again Wynne circled the playroom, grinning happily at Ariadne as she passed her. "This is great fun!" she called to the witch, who waggled her lollipop like a rattle.

Approaching the same boy once more she whispered: "Just follow me. It's important! Hurry!"

Once again he stared at her with a mixture of disbelief and terror. Rather than continuing on around the room, Wynne doubled back and past him again, issuing the same request. She repeated this process twice more, before heading off for a third trip around the room.

On her next approach the boy's shocked expression was waiting for her, plastered across his face like a permanent decoration. "Follow me, or I'll stop playing," she hissed as she passed. She smiled at the rustle of the boy's clothes as he stood and the clatter of his shoes on the stone floor as he followed her. "I'll catch you!" he called in a feeble attempt to make his actions look like part of a game. For the time being, at least, his act seemed to work for no lightning bolts shocked the room into silence.

"I'm here to rescue you all," said Wynne softly as he

drew alongside the scooter, sweat already pouring down his face and glistening in his hair.

"From what?" asked the boy, glancing nervously over his shoulder at Ariadne, who was jumping up and down excitedly at the far end of the room, encouraging a play-fight between two boys.

"From this place, and someone else who's coming here to kidnap some of you."

"Who?"

"My mother," said Wynne, between deep breaths, as the effort of keeping herself in motion took its toll. "She needs children to use in a ritual. She's working for the Pink Witch. Have you heard of the Pink Witch?"

"In horror stories," replied the boy. "Ariadne tells us bedtime stories sometimes so that we lie awake for hours."

"You'll never catch me!" squealed Wynne suddenly, as they drew close to the still hopping Ariadne, and the boy joined in the charade, dropping back a little and making a lame grab for the hem of Wynne's coat. When Ariadne was out of earshot Wynne continued: "I have a plan, but I need your help. A friend of mine, a parradowl is waiting at the west tower for us all. She will get us out somehow, but I have to get everyone there within the next hour and a half. I need you to help me let everyone know without Ariadne hearing."

"You're mad!" The boy stumbled, as if Wynne's revelation had weakened him.

Wynne slowed down a little, hoping her intentions wouldn't be noticed by Ariadne. As the boy caught up again she whispered in her most assertive tone: "Just pass on the word that when I say 'Let's hide everyone!' I want all of you to go to the west tower."

The boy opened his mouth to protest.

"Just do it!" snapped Wynne, and then remembering her manners she asked the boy his name, to which he replied: "It's Joe, I'm an orphan," as if that were his complete title.

"I'm Wynne," she called softly over her shoulder as she headed towards Ariadne, more frightened than she had ever been in her life.

CHAPTER FOURTEEN

1

Ariadne flashed Wynne an uncertain smile, revealing teeth, starkly yellow against the powdery surface of her spoilt face.

"This is great fun!" breathed Wynne, wiping sweat from her forehead, as she scooted around the witch, who twirled in a small circle, keeping her moist blue eyes on the newcomer.

"Keep playing!" came Ariadne's shrill response.

"Oh I will!" Wynne assured her, starting to feel dizzy as she continued to circle the evil school mistress. She saw Joe whispering in the ear of another boy – a small, chubby child wearing black-rimmed glasses. As he spoke he was flaying his arms around, each hand still gripping a character from the farmyard drama.

"Don't you ever want to play too?" Wynne asked Ariadne, changing direction, so as to stop herself feeling sick.

"I do sometimes," replied Ariadne, licking her lolly,

and eyeing Wynne quizzically. "But I get tired."

"What games do you like?"

"I like all games," replied Ariadne, her cracked face suddenly illuminated with enthusiasm. "I like skipping, playing house with dollies, cycling, running, chasing, hiding..."

"Hiding?" Wynne latched upon the word before Ariadne could continue.

"Yes," said the witch, grinning stupidly with the memory of some ancient game. "I like to be It. But I get too irritated when I can't find people now, so I never play it."

A low hum of whispering had broken out in the playroom as news of Wynne's plan circulated.

"When did you last play hide and seek?" she asked hurriedly, desperate to distract Ariadne's attention from the sound.

"Years ago," sighed Ariadne, giving her lolly another consolatory slurp.

"Wouldn't you like to play again?"

"I'll just get grumpy," insisted Ariadne, stamping one of her white-sandaled feet.

"Not if I help you," said Wynne, drawing closer, as if imparting a secret. "I could find out where everyone was planning to hide and give you a really big clue to make it easier."

Ariadne looked thoughtful. She stopped twirling and stood with one long white finger pressed to her chin.

"Maybe," she said finally.

Wynne glanced over the witch's shoulder. The children were playing as before, but she detected a sense of excitement amongst them. Joe had carried out her orders.

"I'll let you think about it," said Wynne cheerfully, pushing off towards Joe, who had returned to his farmyard by the window. As she passed him he gave her a quick, almost undetectable, nod. Wynne felt a rush of excitement and apprehension.

2

Damon clutched the chest containing the Witch Mother's copy of the spell and, he had discovered on opening it, a dagger wrapped in a black cloth, a small jar of what looked like salt, and several black candles. Despite his state of panic after escaping the Pink Witch's home he had remembered to return to the branch where he had left the chest. He also still had the Pink Witch's book safely tucked in the waistband of his trousers. He pushed the chest inside his jumper, which he tucked into his trousers, leaving his hands free to hold the bottom of Toshi's legs. He felt more secure this way. Below him the tree tops of the forest, which grew more wild the further they flew, sped past in a stream of greens, reds and browns. His breath billowed from his mouth, forming clouds in the chill, early evening air.

"All right, boy?" asked Toshi, who had been silent for the best part of the hour since they had escaped the Pink Witch's house.

"Fine!" called Damon. He didn't need to be consoled by a giant bird. But the memory of the Pink Witch crawling in the ashes of the fire and of the clutching hot claws of the fire demon made him shudder.

"Cold?" asked Toshi.

"I'm fine!" snapped Damon.

Toshi tutted at Damon's abrupt tone. "I need to rest for a few minutes," he announced, suddenly sweeping downwards. Damon closed his eyes as they plunged through the canopy of trees, wincing as leaves and twigs brushed and scratched at his face.

It was a relief to feel solid ground beneath his feet, however, and he took the opportunity to stretch his legs while Toshi waddled around pecking in the dirt.

Damon didn't wander far – even the company of a fat red and white bird was preferable to none in the dense and almost silent forest. The atmosphere was cold and dank. He wrapped his arms around his torso, shivering. His jumper offered inadequate protection now that night was closing in.

Damon could hear Toshi tutting as he searched in the ground for titbits to eat. Despite finding the thought of prodding in the ground for grubs to eat repellent, Damon was suddenly aware of his own empty stomach and how empty it felt. He recalled shouting at his mother about the breakfast she had laid out for him on the day he had crossed over into this strange world, and, much to his annoyance, he felt like crying. He wondered what his mother was doing now. Had he burned the house down? Was he dead in his own world? Or was the other Damon enjoying a much more pleasant life than he had been used to here? This concept made Damon prickle with jealousy.

He was still thinking of his mother and feeling tearful when he tripped on something hard and unyielding, partially hidden amongst the fallen leaves on the forest floor. Winded, he swivelled into a sitting position and glared accusingly at the patch of ground where he had tripped. Instead of a large tree root or fallen branch he saw a foot, clad in a bulky, worn brown leather boot. The foot, which had a companion

129

dressed identically, led to a thick-set leg, swathed in dark, earth-stained material. Damon followed the limb to a torso, propped against a tree, the material of the jacket and other layers that covered it almost blending with the bark. Finally, his eyes fell upon the stranger's face, which was as weather-beaten and discoloured by the natural grime of the forest as his clothes. A thick beard covered much of the man's face, whose eyes were closed. Tangled hair fell across his high forehead and sprouted from the nostrils of his bulbous nose. His hands rested in his lap, the nails thick with earth, the lines of his palms like dirt tracks.

"Clumsy," said the man in a soft but powerful voice, without opening his eyes or stirring in any noticeable way.

"Stupid place to sit," returned Damon, studying himself for injuries. His ankles were already raw and sensitive from his brush with the fire demon.

"I've been here five years without causing anyone else any offence." Still the man remained in complete composure.

"Five years," scoffed Damon, standing with much grunting and sighing.

"And three months," added the man.

"Rubbish!"

"Quite true, actually."

"You'd be dead."

"I'm clearly not."

"Well then you clearly haven't been sitting there for five years!" But inspecting the stranger's clothes more carefully, seeing the growth of moss and the teaming life forms that squirmed and scuttled amongst the folds and creases, Damon began to wonder.

"Why would anyone want to sit in a forest for five years?"

"To get away from people who ask questions."

"Very funny."

"And from people who think I'm trying to amuse them when, in fact, I'm being perfectly serious."

Damon mouthed the man's last sentence, screwing

up his face contemptuously.

"And from disrespectful little boys from other worlds," added the man, and Damon felt the colour drain from his face.

"What...how...?" he spluttered.

"Should I expect a complete sentence at some point?" asked the man.

"How did you know about that?" demanded Damon.

"That's what comes of sitting in a wood for five years," replied the man. "You become sensitive to such things." A large black beetle crawled slowly across his face as he spoke, but he didn't so much as twitch his nose.

"What about food?" asked Damon. "And, well, other things that people have to do?"

"I haven't eaten, so I don't need to do the other things."

"Aren't you hungry?"

"I was for the first two or three years, but then I got used to it."

"You must be like a skeleton." Damon tried to detect the man's body through the layers of clothing.

"Not at all. I feed on the energy of nature."

Damon scowled. "Wouldn't you rather have a hamburger and fries?"

"A what?"

"Never mind. Has anyone else been past here recently?" Damon was thinking of the Witch Mother.

"No. You're the first in three years. Although someone is approaching from the south. A woman, I think, and a man. They've got a horse and cart with them and their intent is evil. She seems familiar, actually, but I can't picture her clearly yet."

"It's the Witch Mother!" gasped Damon. "How close are they?"

"They should pass by in about ten minutes," said the man. "I can see them now...Oh no!"

Suddenly the man's eyes snapped open, wide and panic-stricken. "I have to go," he announced, leaping to his feet and stumbling off through the trees, his legs buckling every few paces like those of a new-born fawn.

Damon stared after him and shook his head, then remembering his own predicament, he raced back to Toshi. The bird was still pecking in the dirt, tutting contentedly to himself.

"We have to go!" yelled Damon, skidding to a halt inches from where Toshi was foraging. "The Witch Mother is almost here."

"How do you know that?" asked Toshi, cocking his head to eye Damon.

"A smelly man who lives under a tree told me. Come on!"

With a loud, disgruntled tut, Toshi began to flap his great wings.

"Hurry!" Damon was sure he could hear the creaking of the Witch Mother's cart and the crack of the dishevelled servant's whip.

And then he saw the motley group through the trees:

Barrow the horse plodding slowly onwards, his large head hanging sadly, the Witch Mother perched just behind, the Pink Witch's servant leading the horse, his spindle-legs sagging with fatigue.

Toshi saw them too and grabbed Damon by his jumper, flapping his wings more urgently. They began to rise and for a moment Damon thought they would escape undetected.

"What are you doing here?" came the strident screech of the Witch Mother. "You horrible, inconvenient little brat."

They rose slowly towards the forest roof, Damon aware of his legs still dangling close to the ground. "What's wrong with you?" he screamed at Toshi.

"I'm tired," rasped Toshi, trying to muster the energy to propel them upwards.

"We'll be dead if you don't try harder!" Damon glanced back and saw the Witch Mother rising from her perch, arms outstretched as if to embrace someone of whom she was not overly fond.

"What's she doing?" whispered Damon, as a fluttering sound began to fill the wood. "What's that?"

Toshi gave a defiant tut and they shot upwards, Damon's face distorted by the force. The fluttering sound grew more intense and a dark mass suddenly surrounded them. At first Damon thought it must be smoke conjured by the Witch Mother to choke them or steer them off course. It followed them through the tree tops and into open sky, the fluttering sound filling Damon's head. And then he saw hundreds of piercing little eyes and thousands of tiny, gnashing teeth.

"Bats!" he cried, as leathery wings beat against his cheeks.

CHAPTER FIFTEEN

1

"Bats!" Damon shrieked again, flapping his hands wildly in front of his face, scattering soft, fat bodies. "Get me away from here!" he cried. "I hate bats. Get me away from here!"

"I'm trying," rasped Toshi, who was beating his wings against the tide of flying rodents.

Pin-sharp teeth dug into Damon's arms and legs, hooked claws raked at the skin. "Please!" he begged, losing all his usual arrogance. He felt them crawling up his back and tangling themselves in his hair. He tore them free, flinging them towards the ground. He watched them drop like grenades. But then he saw them rise again, evil eyes fixed on his, hungry for another taste of his blood.

"Toshi, fly higher, you idiot!"

"I'm trying!" repeated the exasperated bird, but the bats were attacking him too, lodging themselves amongst his thick feathers, hanging onto his wings like ugly charms.

Damon suddenly remembered the small chest of magic paraphernalia tucked inside his jumper. He pulled it out, fumbling for the catch, trying to block out the pain and repulsion he was feeling. The lid popped open and Damon's hand delved inside searching for the dagger. He freed it from its black wrapping and brandished it before him, slicing at the thick black cloud of bats. He heard shrieks, saw flecks of red before his eyes like stars and felt warm blood spatter across his face. He began to slice the attacking swarm indiscriminately, wincing as the blade cut their blood-bloated bellies or sliced through their beating wings.

"Wait!" cried Toshi. "I can get through now. Stop!"

But Damon continued to attack, beginning to enjoy the killing, to relish in the small explosion as each body burst open.

"Stop!" called Toshi again, and he shot forward, bat bodies dropping on every side.

They quickly out-flew the remaining bats. Damon pulled the last few from his clothes and hair and flung them

138

downwards. The diminished cloud behind them soon dispersed, diving back into the trees. Below them the Witch Mother, invisible beneath the canopy of the forest, was cursing and hitting the Pink Witch's servant with a small branch.

Damon let out a triumphant whoop as they sped on towards the Pentagram School. Toshi was silent for a moment and when he spoke his voice was brimming with anger.

"You didn't need to kill so many," he said. "I told you I could get through them, but you kept killing."

"They were attacking us!" protested Damon, wiping blood from the dagger and returning it to the chest, which he shoved back up his jumper. "They were only bats."

"Blackwing is a bat. A giant talking bat, but a bat. Blackwing is my closest friend."

"You eat rats, don't you? Anyway, they were attacking us!" repeated Damon, his voice high with indignation.

"They were being controlled by your mother. Bats don't normally attack parradowls and nasty little boys. And as for rats, they're vermin."

"Well I hate bats," hissed Damon. "And that witch is not my mother!"

They flew on in silence.

2

"I do want to play hide and seek," announced Ariadne, appearing at Wynne's side. Relieved, Wynne brought the scooter to a halt. She could barely feel her legs after half an hour of constant scooting.

"Great!" she enthused. "How long are you going to give us to hide?"

"No,' laughed Ariadne. "I'm not being It on my own. I thought of this myself – we're both going to be It." Ariadne leaned closer to Wynne, cupping her withered hands around her mouth and placing them close to Wynne's ear. "That means you can help me and I won't get grumpy," she whispered.

"Right," said Wynne, desperately trying to think of a way around this chink in her plan.

"Come on then!" squealed Ariadne, waving her lollipop, which glowed like a traffic light, until the attention of every child was focused on her. "We're going to play a new game," she announced. "So you can stop playing whatever game you're playing now."

A huge communal sigh of relief filled the room, as children flopped to the floor or leaned against walls, some hugging each other tearfully.

Ariadne's happy expression faltered for a second.

"Tell them about hide and seek," Wynne encouraged.

"I will!" snapped the witch, and then the grin returned to her hideous clown-face. "I'm going to count to ten..." she began.

"Ten!" exclaimed Wynne. "Where's the fun in that? They won't have time to get out of this room."

"Out of this room?" Ariadne looked mystified.

"You do want this to be fun, don't you?" asked Wynne.

"All right, I'll count to twenty."

"One hundred," suggested Wynne.

"I'll never find them!" insisted Ariadne, stamping her foot.

"We'll find them together," Wynne assured her. "The longer we give them to hide the more fun it will be for us. Every time we find one of them they can help us look for the others. It will be over in a flash."

"You'd better be right," snarled Ariadne, then grinning once more she continued: "I'll count to seventy-five and then this girl and I will come looking for you. If I haven't found you all in twenty minutes I want you to come back here and carry on playing with the toys. Is that clear?'

"Yes," cried all the children, smiling for the first time since Wynne's arrival.

"Shall we close our eyes then?" said Wynne.

"Why?" asked Ariadne, wrinkling her flaky nose.

"So that we don't see which way they go," replied Wynne, as if talking to a small child.

Ariadne's shoulders slumped and she stomped over to the nearest wall, lollipop dangling at her side. "One! Two! Three!..."

Wynne ushered the children towards the door that led to the entrance hall and with a chorus of excited shrieks and yelps they were gone.

"Forty-nine!" bellowed Ariadne.

"You can't be up to forty-nine yet." Wynne marched over to the witch, She was surprised to see that her eyes were screwed shut.

"I am!" insisted Ariadne. "Fifty-seven!"

"Stop cheating!"

"They won't know."

"That's not the point."

"You said we could cheat. You said you were going to give me a clue."

"I could hardly ask them to tell me where they would

all be hiding when I'm being It with you, could I?"

"I'm starting to get grumpy already," warned Ariadne.

"No need for that. It's going to be the best game ever. Now let's be fair and start from one,"

"No way!"

"Twenty then," said Wynne hastily.

"Forty!"

"All right, forty."

And as they began to count towards seventy-five, Wynne prayed that the other children would reach the west tower before Ariadne caught them and that Heeshee would have thought of a way of getting them out of the school. She also prayed that she would think of a way of escaping herself, which at the moment seemed very unlikely.

"Forty-one!" boomed Ariadne. "Forty-two!"

CHAPTER SIXTEEN

1

"Seventy-five!" cried Ariadne excitedly, leaping in the air and twisting round to face into the playroom. "Which way should we go? Which way should we go?"

Wynne turned in a far more subdued fashion and nodded towards the door through which the children had left. She could see no point in lying, surely even Ariadne must have heard the commotion of their exit.

"This way then!" shrieked the witch, flinging the door open and running into the hall, where she stood twirling in a circle like a dog chasing its tail, yelping: "Where now? Where now?"

All Wynne could think about was how she was going to get away from Ariadne and join the other children in the west tower. She wasn't even sure how to get there. Heeshee had flapped a wing at it outside, but Wynne felt so completely disorientated after circling the play room hundreds of times she had lost all sense of direction.

"Upstairs?" asked Ariadne. "Downstairs? Which room? Oh this is ridiculously difficult. I knew this was a bad idea. We should have insisted they all hid in the same place. How are we supposed to find thirty-odd children all in different hiding places all over the school?"

"If only you knew," thought Wynne, but out loud she said with faked boundless energy: "I think we should try upstairs first. That's where I'd hide. And if we really can't find them, they'll all be back in the playroom in twenty minutes."

"If they're not, I'll just use some magic to flush them out," said Ariadne. "Maybe I should do that anyway."

"No!" Wynne placed a hand on Ariadne's arm, which felt like cold bone. "Let's try and play without using magic. It'll be much more fun."

"Come on then,' conceded Ariadne, stomping up the wide, curved stairway. Life-size wax works of nursery rhyme characters lined either side of the stairs – Red Riding Hood was sitting on the left hand banister, clutching a basket and eating a cake meant for grandmother; the wolf was a little further up, its shaggy head peering between two spindles, its lithe body, coiled round another. Running down the stairs towards them, frozen on the fourth stair down was Cinderella, minus one glass slipper and just behind her a dismayed Prince Charming.

"This is lovely," said Wynne.

"It makes me happy," said Ariadne, obviously pleased by Wynne's admiration.

They reached the first landing, where Wynne stood looking from side to side, torn between her desire to join the other children and the need to keep Ariadne away from them.

"Where now?" demanded Ariadne, shifting her weight from one foot to the other.

"This way," said Wynne, heading down a corridor to their left, which she hoped led to the eastern side of the school, although having no perception of which way north was, she couldn't be sure. Doors lined each side of the corridor, which was painted bright white like the playroom and the hall, and was decorated with stencils of leaping pixies.

"Aren't they sweet!" Ariadne prodded one of the painted fairy folk with her lolly, grinning impishly. The drawing sprang to life, waving back at the witch and smiling fixedly.

"They are cute," said Wynne. "Shall we try in this room? I think I may have heard breathing." Wynne rested her hand on the brass knob of the first door. Ariadne nodded madly. Wynne pressed a finger to her lips and pushed the door open.

Beyond lay another long passage, the walls lined with shelves, all crammed full of toys. Some looked brand new, others worn and broken. It was like an immense attic stuffed with forgotten childhood friends. With raised eyebrows, Wynne pressed on, hoping she would not be buried beneath an avalanche of dolls and teddy bears. Ariadne skipped behind her, obviously not yet turning grumpy.

"Is anybody there?" the witch called in a comically doom-filled voice. "Coming, ready or not!"

Wynne pretended to peer beneath the shelves in search of hiding children, regularly throwing smiles at Ariadne to show she was enjoying this new game. For now, Ariadne was smiling back.

The passageway came to an abrupt end at another door, which Wynne pulled open.

"Maybe there'll be some hiding through here," she said.

"I hope so," said Ariadne, and Wynne detected a hint of disgruntlement.

The door led to a flight of stairs, which Wynne prayed did not lead to the west tower. She took them one at a time, prolonging the tension. She need not have worried. After seven steps she found herself standing in a large bright room.

"My bedroom," announced Ariadne.

It couldn't have been anything else. A four-poster bed, big enough for ten people to sleep in it comfortably together, stood in the centre of the room. Heavy purple velvet curtains were pulled across each side, red bows sown into the fabric every few inches. The bedspread was, at first glance, a traditional patchwork quilt, but approaching from the doorway, Wynne saw that each patch included a scene from a nursery rhyme or fairy tale. There in the bottom right hand corner was Humpty Dumpty, fat face smiling, disproportionate legs dangling over a towering wall. Just entering the square in the very bottom corner of the quilt was a line of mounted soldiers – an ominous hint of what was to befall the jovial egg. Next to the doomed Humpty's square was a patch featuring a beautiful white-skinned woman, reposing in a glass coffin, surrounded by seven miserable little men and next to this square a detailed tableau of a young girl and boy climbing a bright green hill, a bucket swinging between them, oblivious to their imminent fate. Wynne realised how cruel nursery stories actually were. They made her gloomy life seem almost pleasant.

The floor of the room was covered with dolls, some life-size, others bigger than life-size, their beady eyes staring or gently closed, depending on their posture. Each doll was dressed in the most girlish of clothes – lace, bows and silver buckles were the fashion of this pretend child's world. The dolls, all two hundred or more, were beautiful. But as Wynne surveyed their reclining, sitting and standing forms, she shivered.

"There's no one in here," said Ariadne, and Wynne jumped, for a second thinking one of the eerily composed dolls had spoken.

"No," she agreed, turning to retrace their steps.

"I'm bored with this," announced Ariadne, clasping one of the smaller dolls to her chest for comfort.

"We have to try for a bit longer." Wynne, tugged at the witch's arm, but Ariadne was sinking into a sulk.

"I said I'm bored," she insisted, her mouth screwed up very small.

"But we've barely started," said Wynne cheerily.

"I want the children to start playing again," said Ariadne darkly. "I think this was just a way for them to rest. This isn't a game at all is it? They're all in their dormitory sleeping, aren't they?"

"No, they're definitely not there," Wynne assured her.

"I bet they are!" Ariadne's white dress turned black as she pushed past Wynne and stormed down the steps to the passage of toys. "I'll teach them!" she shrieked. "I'll make them play until they drop dead!"

Wynne watched after the deranged mistress. She was surprised, and relieved, that she hadn't been punished immediately for her part in the scheme.

A cold, hard hand touched her shoulder and a tinny, girlish voice said: "Time to play for keeps."

And as Wynne turned to face the child-size doll, it's glass eyes filled with hatred, she realised Ariadne planned to punish her more than any of the other children.

CHAPTER SEVENTEEN

1

For a moment horror kept Wynne rigid, staring into the bright blue of the doll's eyes. The eerie feeling that had swept through her on first looking at the dolls intensified as the pretty blonde head turned from side to side, creaking as if the joint needed oiling. "Time to play for keeps!" she said again, and Wynne saw smaller bodies closing in around her, as all the dolls began to stir. Those that had been sleeping sat up, their hate-filled eyes snapping open, those that were standing began to walk with unbending legs, their little hands reaching out for a deadly hug.

Wynne took a step backwards towards the door and the largest doll followed. "Time to play for keeps! Time to play for keeps!" The other dolls joined in her chant, as they walked, crawled and rolled towards her, like demon babies. Wynne fumbled behind her for the door handle. She felt something crawl across her foot and screamed kicking the small prettily dressed doll with teeth like needles across the room. As soon as its hard little body hit the floor it rolled over and began to crawl towards her, grinning like a devil.

Wynne turned with another scream and ran down the small flight of stairs. The corridor was swathed in darkness and around her soft teddy limbs were twitching, wooden soldiers stirring and devil dolls reaching their smooth pink hands through the piles of other toys. "Time to play for keeps!" the chant began to rise like the buzzing of a hive from the shelves as the toys came to life.

Wynne ran, arms close to her sides so that she would not touch any of the squirming bodies as they groped for the edge of the shelves, reaching for her in the darkness. Stuffed bodies dropped to the floor, wooden legs began to march, cry-baby dolls to crawl after her, wailing the chorus: "Time to play for keeps! Time to play for keeps!"

Finally, Wynne fell against the door leading to the first landing and flung it open, leaping from the claustrophobic confines of the corridor. Gasping for breath she slammed the door behind her, ignoring the screams of agitated toys deprived of their game. It would only be a matter of time before one of the larger dolls arrived to turn the handle, or the combined strength of hundreds of depraved playthings forced it open.

The landing, too, was in darkness. Wynne felt her way along the nearest wall, listening for evidence of other predators. She needed to find the west tower while Ariadne was searching the dormitory for her deceitful pupils. Her hands suddenly touched the glass pane of a window and a surge of magic shot through her body. She yelped and leapt backwards. As she blew on her singed hands she heard the padding of soft feet and the breathing of a large animal just feet away. Images played through her mind – a huge demonic teddy bear with deadly claws, a stuffed toy dog with real fangs that could tear her to pieces. And then she remembered the wolf. She knew as soon as she pictured its dirty brown body coiled around the spindles of the stairway that this was the creature that stalked her.

She continued to shuffle along the wall, barely containing the sobs that were bursting to leap from her quivering mouth. In the darkness, nearer than before, she heard the wolf snarl. Soon she would feel its hot breath on her arm and then its huge jaws closing around her hand. But instead of teeth dripping saliva, it was a feminine, cold hand that took hold of Wynne's and rather than the rattling, wet growl of the animal, a soft, musical voice whispered: "This way!" and she was pulled along the corridor, almost stumbling as they went.

The wolf howled angrily and Wynne heard its claws clicking on the stone floor as it gave chase.

Light suddenly flooded the passageway as a door opened just ahead, Wynne glancing backwards, saw the agile beast bounding towards her, its tongue lolling from its vicious jaws. It skidded to a halt and crouched bearing its pink gums as it snarled, ready to pounce. Wynn's new friend yanked her through the door. Wynne tripped, just managing to slap her hands to the floor to break the fall. She heard the door slam shut and the howl of the wolf as it hit the other side.

Wynne turned to thank her protector, but the words caught in her throat and instead she stared in amazement at the girl who stood with her back to the door, smiling down at her. She was dressed in a red cape, the hood of which covered her auburn hair, but for a single lock that hung across her pale forehead. Her cheeks were bright red, as if she had just taken a vigorous walk and in her right hand she carried a wicker basket.

"It can't be," whispered Wynne.

"Are you all right?" asked Red Riding Hood.

2

Damon and Toshi arrived at the Pentagram School some fifteen minutes after fighting their way through the bats. Toshi had maintained a moody silence during the flight, unbroken by the still sulking Damon. Toshi quickly spotted Heeshee perched on a high window ledge on the west tower and swooped down to join her. He deposited Damon on the narrow ledge that ran all the way round the outside of the tower and immediately began to tut and tweet at his wife, whose feathers puffed-up lovingly at the sight of him.

"Hello!" snapped Damon. "Aren't we supposed to be rescuing orphans or something?"

Heeshee tensed, her feathers deflating instantly. She turned her angry eyes on Damon, who shrank back a little, aware of just how dangerous the bird's beak could be. "I have been rescuing children," she said tersely. "If you'd just take the time to look down there into the trees you will see thirty-two of them huddled together in a clump of bushes, waiting for you and your sister to lead them to safety."

"Where is Wynne?" asked Damon, forgetting to mention that she was not his real sister.

"She hasn't turned up yet. A very nice boy called Joe, who is indeed an orphan, said that she had last been seen in the very unwelcome company of Ariadne the Awful, who he said very much lived up to her name…"

158

"So she's still in there somewhere?" Damon tried not to sound concerned.

"Yes," Heeshee glanced through the small arched window, the only window not protected by magic. A hundred feet below there was a pile of rubble where the stone steps and the floor of the room in the top of the tower had crumbled. She had breathed a sigh of relief when the first of the children had crawled through the partly obscured entrance, choking on dust, peering hopefully up at the window. She had carried each one to safety, telling them to wait quietly in the forest until Wynne was there to lead them to a safe place. As time ticked on she had grown increasingly agitated. Soon the Witch Mother would arrive and rather than saving the children from her, Heeshee realised she would have made obtaining them easier than if they had been left in the school. She doubted the Witch Mother would have much trouble gaining entrance to the establishment. It wasn't powerful magic that held the children prisoner – it didn't need to be. A simple counter spell from even the most inadequate witch would be enough to create an accessible window. Ariadne had never had to worry about anyone breaking into the school. As long as the children kept coming and playing, she was happy.

A small cry and the sound of rubble being disturbed from below jolted Heeshee to full alertness. She peered into the dark tower and saw several shadowy forms crawling over the pile of stone.

"Heeshee!"

It was Wynne.

Damon leaned through the window, his face pressed against Heeshee's, her feathers tickling his cheek.

"Wynne!" he called, forgetting to act like a brat.

"Damon? Damon help us. There's four of us down here and there's a very angry witch, a wolf and lots of horrible toys after us."

"Start blocking the entrance with stones," called Heeshee, We'll get you out."

Heeshee dived down to fulfil her promise and Toshi

hastily followed, breathing in so as to squeeze through the narrow window. Damon, forced to step to one side to let the birds through, regained his place at the window, trying to decipher Wynne in the almost pitch darkness of the tower.

Heeshee reached the four escapees first as they struggled to climb the pile of rocks, their faces caked in grey flecks. Her excellent vision made out two women, one dressed in a red cape, the other in what looked like a ball gown. Behind her came the dishevelled form of a man – a very handsome man with black hair and a noble high forehead. As he climbed he was pushing large pieces of stone back down the pile so that they blocked the entrance. Through the remaining gap Heeshee saw a crowd gathering and heard a mixture of snarls and high-pitched wails.

"Take them first!" breathed Wynne, as Heeshee made a grab for her filthy coat. For a second the bird hesitated.

"Please!" insisted Wynne.

Toshi had already begun his ascent, carrying the red

caped girl in his talons. She seemed relatively calm, wiping dust from her bare knees as she rose.

Heeshee flew to the other woman, searching for a piece of cloth that she could grip hold of on the strapless gown. Finally she hooked her talons through the woman's thick yellow hair, which was piled on top of her head, and hoisted her towards the window. The woman screamed with pain, but Heeshee had no time for such nonsense.

A hand was reaching through the small gap that the man hadn't managed to cover with rock. In it was clasped a large red lollipop.

"It's her!" the man whispered desperately. "She'll turn us to wax-works again."

Wynne grabbed for a piece of stone and flung it at the white, weathered hand. With a scream Ariadne dropped the lollipop and snatched her hand back through the gap. "Get it!" called Wynne scrambling down the mountain of rubble. The man made a frantic grab for the magical sweet, but Toshi, unaware of recent events caught him by the collar of his jacket and lifted him into the air. Wynne continued to crawl towards the lollipop, eyes stinging and weeping from the cloud of dust. Above her Damon was straining to see what was going on. Heeshee and Toshi were in the woods, dropping off their charges, leaving Damon alone on the ledge.

He heard Wynne scream and knew that she was in terrible danger. He glanced down to where Toshi and Heeshee were preparing to take flight, but Wynne's screams sounded too urgent to wait for the return of the birds and without giving himself time to reconsider, Damon leapt through the window, dropping towards the ground, air whistling in his ears. He was falling, not flying. Then with a weird jerk he found himself suspended in mid-air, just inches from the ground. Heart pounding he searched for Wynne. He saw her lying in the rubble, hands clutching what appeared to be a dirty lollipop.

And gnawing its way up the stick of the lolly, phlegm spraying in every direction, was a wolf, its great shaggy head forcing its way through what remained of the entrance, its wild eyes blazing, as it chewed its way towards Wynn's hands.

Damon picked up a handful of rubble and flung it into the wolf's face. The creature howled and stopped chewing, but it did not retract its head. Wynne was tugging at the lollipop, as if it were the most important thing in the world. Damon decided to trust her judgement. He alighted on top of the rubble mountain and picked up a large slab of stone, groaning with the effort. He held it above the wolf's head and, closing his eyes so as not to witness the carnage, he let it drop. A loud crack and a sickening squelch announced his success. Wynne gave a shocked cry and crawled away from the messy results of Damon's quick thinking. In her hand she held the lollipop.

"You must really be hungry," said Damon, as Toshi and Heeshee zoomed into view, their bright feathers back-lit by brilliant moonlight.

CHAPTER EIGHTEEN

1

The Witch Mother was still fuming from her encounter with

Damon as Brackwell tugged on Barrow's reins, bringing the

tired horse to a halt on the edge of the clearing where the

Pentagram School stood.

"What was he doing so far into the woods with a

Parradowl?" she asked the servant for the fifteenth time. He

gave his skeletal shoulders a barely noticeable shrug by

way of a reply and held out his gnarled hand to the angry

witch. For a moment she looked confusedly at the proffered

palm, unused to anyone offering her assistance, then pushing

it to one side, she jumped from her seat landing like a

gymnast on the forest floor.

"Don't mention anything about that little brat to your

mistress, will you?" she asked the servant, voice shaky.

Brackwell shook his head, face expressionless.

"Wait for ten minutes then bring the cart up to the

school with the back end facing whichever window you see me climb through," said the Witch Mother. Brackwell nodded and the Witch Mother nodded back, still not comfortable giving orders to another adult. "Right," she said. "I'll get this done then."

Feeling just a little of the apprehension her daughter had felt hours earlier, the Witch Mother followed the path lined with dead trees to the Pentagram School. She didn't head for the front door, but veered to the left, stopping in front of a large arched window, beyond which lay the playroom.

"I'd better let her know I'm here," she muttered, taking a crystal ball, the size of a small apple from her cardigan pocket. She rubbed the smooth surface with her free hand and whispered "Agnes the Pink Witch." The ball began to glow and issue a low hum. Seconds later the Pink Witch's face appeared, distorted like the reflection in the convex surface of a spoon.

"What?" demanded the other witch, wiping chocolate

from around her mouth."

"I'm here," whispered the Witch Mother.

"Well get inside and snatch some children. Why are you bothering me? I'm having my wig re-styled. I'll see you later."

The crystal cleared and the Witch Mother returned it to her pocket with a sigh.

From the same pocket she took a piece of white chalk and drew a line around the window frame, standing on tip-toe so as to reach above the pointed top, crouching to draw beneath it. The line complete, she stepped backwards, spread her arms and recited a short incantation. As she spoke the chalk outline began to glow and as she completed the spell and clapped her hands the entire window slid to one side, leaving a perfect arch-shaped hole.

"Well done Agnes – a spell for every occasion," she whispered, as she climbed through the magic entrance with her usual agility. Brackwell watched her disappear, his expression even more dismal than usual.

The playroom was in complete darkness. The Witch Mother held up the piece of chalk and whispered another simple spell, causing the chalk to glow, shedding a sombre light that reached barely three feet ahead. It stretched far enough to light the crouched form of a woman, huddled by the door of the playroom. The Witch Mother froze. Even she knew the reputation of Ariadne the Awful – and surely this woman with shaggy blond hair pouring across her shoulders and down her back was Ariadne. She was in a sorry state, however, her white dress stained grey, her skin scratched and bleeding. She stirred as the Witch Mother watched, slowly turning to look into the light of the chalk. As she lifted her face to stare at the intruder, the Witch Mother gave an involuntary cry and stumbled backwards.

"They left me," sobbed the creature, whose skin was as grey as her clothes, hanging from the bones like loose elephant hide. "They stopped playing!" As she crawled across the playroom floor clumps of yellow hair dropped from her head, revealing patches of grey-white scalp. "They

168

stopped playing!" Now her teeth were falling out, bloody roots bright against the white floor.

"Help me!" she wailed, reaching out a quivering hand.

"Get away," hissed the Witch Mother edging back towards the window, but as she glared at the shaking hand it crumbled like old plaster and in front of her stunned eyes, the rest of Ariadne the Awful began to crack and fall away from her bones. The Witch Mother gave a startled yelp as the other witch's jaw bone clattered to the floor. And soon there was nothing left of Ariadne the Awful, Ariadne the terrifying overgrown child, Ariadne the three hundred year-old mistress of the once world-renowned Pentagram School, other than a pile of dust.

2

At the time the Witch Mother was approaching the school, Wynne, Damon and the thirty-five escapees were emerging into a small clearing three miles into the forest. Damon was furious that no-one had thanked him properly for his part in the rescue and was lagging some way behind as the other children and the three fairytale characters threw their exhausted bodies onto the damp grass. Heeshee and Toshi joined them, equally glad to rest their tired wings.

"We'll have to go soon, dearie," Heeshee chirped in Wynne's ear.

"Really?" Wynne turned her dusty and mud-stained face towards her feathered friend.

"Got my own babies to think about ," said the bird. "Just keep trekking in this direction for another twenty miles and you'll come to the village of Misty Well. They look after children there. There's a kind witch, Belinda the Beautiful, who's actually quite plain, but has a lovely personality. She's not as powerful as the Pink Witch, but there's enough magic in Misty Well for that ghastly woman not to bother her. She'll give all these children a place to live. A lot of Lightsleep's children end up there. Some get lost on the way and end up in terrible places like that school or even worse the Circus…"

"Come on dear." Toshi gave his wife a gentle peck. "Blackwing will be worried. You know he gets nervous when he babysits for more than a couple of hours."

"I know, I know." Heeshee rubbed her soft head against Wynne's cheek. "Take care dearie, and get these children to Misty Well and Belinda the Beautiful."

"I will." Tears were streaming down Wynne's face as Heeshee hopped away and then took off, her loving husband close behind.

"Yeah, bye!'" called Damon, sarcastically, stomping over to where Wynne was lying. "Nice of them to remember me," he said, flopping onto the ground next to her.

"They were worried about their eggs," said Wynne. "It was good of them to see us this far. We can't rest for long, just in case the Witch Mother decides to give chase."

"She won't catch us. Did you see how slowly that cart was moving through the trees?"

"Maybe she'll leave the cart and come after us just for the sake of it," said Wynne. "She might not be the most powerful witch, but when she gets really angry she sometimes manages to do things she never dreamed she could do."

"Like what?"

Before Wynne could answer Red Riding Hood came skipping over to them, smiling radiantly.

"This place reminds me of home!" she cried in her sing-song voice. "I used to gather edible berries in the woods near my house, until the wolf started making a nuisance of himself."

"Why don't you gather some now?" asked Damon. "I'm starving."

"Maybe we could look for some on the way," suggested Wynne. "We've got a long way to go and the Witch Mother isn't far behind."

"I'll form a little gathering party," said Red Riding Hood skipping off again.

"Is she really..." began Damon.

"I think so," said Wynne.

"And them?" Damon nodded at the blonde haired woman in the ball gown, and the tall dark man who were arguing at the edge of the clearing.

"I didn't ask you to come chasing after me," shouted the red-faced woman.

"Oh, so all that flirty chat and those coy looks were meant to give me some other impression, were they?"

"Oh shut up! Don't you think we've got more important things to worry about?"

"Not quite like in the book," whispered Wynne. "Do you have the same stories in your world?"

"I think so." Damon frowned at the irate Cinderella and Prince Charming.

"What do we do with them?" asked Wynne.

"I don't know. Where did they come from?"

"I was talking to Red Riding Hood – her name's Samantha – and she said that she remembers walking through the woods on the way to her grandmother's house, and seeing the wolf skulking after her, when suddenly she was in the school and Ariadne the Awful was skipping round her like a deranged child. Apparently she made Samantha act out the story of Red Riding Hood about ten times without the real wolf then got bored and summoned the wolf, too, and watched while it chased Samantha round the school. Samantha says she was getting really good at getting away from it when Ariadne said she was bored again. The next thing she knew she was waking up on the stairway where I first saw her. She saved my life."

"That's so weird!" Damon sat up and glared at Cinderella and her prince, whose arguing was growing increasingly heated.

"And that glass slipper, left on the top step, that was just an accident was it?"

"Yes!" Cinderella marched off into the trees, tripping on the dragging hem of her dress.

The Prince laughed loudly and the belle of his ball

174

threw her remaining glass slipper at his head.

"I don't think they're going to live happily ever after," said Wynne, and Damon laughed. Soon Wynne was chuckling too, then she was looking at Damon strangely.

"What?" Damon stopped laughing and frowned at her.

"Sorry," said Wynne. "You reminded me of the real Damon for a minute. I suppose you are in his body. You're just so different from him usually."

"I am the real Damon!" Damon was about to stomp off in a huff but was distracted by a desperate wail from a little way into the forest. Cinderella suddenly re-emerged into the clearing, hair a frenzy of frizz and curls, dressed in a tatty brown rag and carrying a broom.

"It's midnight!" she announced miserably.

CHAPTER NINETEEN

1

Cinderella shuffled sorrowfully behind the others as they ventured on through the forest, pushing their way through increasingly dense foliage. True to her word, Samantha of the red cape had formed a party of four, including a girl and boy of around ten, and Prince Charming, who kept smiling at Samantha and then glancing coolly over his shoulder at Cinderella. The strange group had managed to fill Samantha's basket with berries, ready for a small feast at their next stopping place. Wynne had taken her place at the head of the trekkers, Damon close behind. Joe, the orphan, was walking beside him, although he had barely spoken a word, except to announce his name and lack of parents. The small girl, called Molly, who Wynne had first seen riding the scooter at the Pentagram School, kept trying to hold Damon's hand, which he found extremely embarrassing, while the plump boy with black-rimmed glasses had proved himself to have an excellent sense of direction.

"That way is north," he instructed Wynne, running to catch up, "so to hit the village of Misty Well – if it's in the direction you originally pointed out to me – we have to change direction slightly." He indicated with a small red hand the way they needed to go.

"Are you sure?" asked Wynne, but one look at his earnest round face and she led the group in the direction he'd suggested.

"My name's George, by the way," said the boy. "My parents left me in the woods three years ago."

"Why?" asked Wynne, horrified.

"Because of her, the Pink Witch. I was born in a village a little way from her house. Every time she saw me walking down the street she'd fire a bolt of magic at me and scream: 'Out of my sight you disgusting little creature!' So my parents thought it would be best all round if I got as far away from her as possible."

"So they just left you in the forest?" exclaimed

Wynne.

"Not exactly. They didn't plan it that way. They didn't have much choice."

"Why?"

"They were eaten by a bear."

"I'm so sorry!" Wynne felt hot with the horror of the revelation and the embarrassment of not knowing how to react. George shrugged and said: "It was a really big bear," as if that made everything easier to accept.

"I think we'll have to stop soon," said Wynne. She was cold, but some of the children looked frozen. She wished she had told them to dress warmly before heading for the west tower. "We should try and make a shelter from branches and get a fire going so that we can get warm."

"What if the Witch Mother sees the smoke?" asked Damon, pushing himself between Wynne and George.

"I think we'll have to risk it," said Wynne, "or risk half of us dying of cold."

Starting a fire proved a lengthy business in the damp atmosphere of the forest. Samantha and Wynne took a small group of children on a search for dry firewood while Damon and a boy called Cameron, who had dark brown skin and large brown eyes, tried to create the embryo of a blaze by rubbing two pieces of stone together over a small pile of twigs. George was peering over their shoulders as they took it in turns to attempt the seemingly impossible task.

"This is useless," sighed Cameron, passing the stones back to Damon. Around them the other children were huddled together for warmth. One or two of the younger escapees were crying, their arms and legs red with cold.

"Can I make a suggestion?" ventured George, taking off his glasses and cleaning them on his white shirt.

"No!" snapped Damon, who had taken a dislike to George, because Wynne seemed fond of him.

"We may as well listen to him," said Cameron, watching Damon's latest unsuccessful attempt to create a spark.

"Well?" Damon looked up at George, not bothering to mask his dislike for the other boy.

"The lolly," said George.

Damon frowned. "What are you talking about?"

"Ariadne's lolly," said George. "She used to shoot lightning from it. I just wondered if we might be able to use it to start a fire."

"Where is it?" demanded Damon, annoyed that George's idea made sense.

"I think your sister has it," replied George. "Shall I go and find her?"

"She has got it," said Joe, from amongst the shivering bunch of children. He looked as sombre here as he did amongst the toys in Ariadne's playroom. "She keeps it in the inside pocket of her coat."

"You've been paying her a lot of attention," said Damon, who didn't like Joe either.

"But I'm wearing her coat," piped up Molly, who

had been dozing with her head on Jo's shoulder. She had tried to sleep leaning against Damon, but he had pushed her away.

"Is the lolly in the pocket?" asked Joe, giving Molly's hair a friendly ruffle.

Molly fumbled inside the coat, which was far too big for her, finally producing the now sorry-looking lollipop.

Damon gave the dirt-encrusted sweet a dour look as he took it from Molly, holding it between finger and thumb like something infectious.

"What do I do with it now?" he asked.

"Shall I try?" asked George, reaching out a chubby hand, but Damon stood up abruptly, snatching the lolly away.

"Try pointing it at the twigs and saying fire," suggested Cameron, who also stood, rubbing his arms, which were a mass of goose bumps.

Damon felt slightly stupid holding out a ruined lollipop and screaming "fire" at a pile of twigs, but he tried it anyway, blushing at the complete lack of response. The huddled children gave a communal despondent moan.

"Let me try," said George, reaching again for the lolly.

"No!" shouted Damon, his face contorted with anger, and a small bolt of lightning shot from the lolly, bouncing off the twigs and shooting straight up, finally fading in the air like dying fireworks.

"Wow!" gasped Cameron, staring at the now smouldering twigs. "You did it."

"Yeah," said Damon nonchalantly, putting his hands behind his back to hide the fact that they were shaking.

A loud scream broke the tension.

"Wynne?" Damon stared into the gloom of the forest. The scream came again, nearer than before, and Wynne broke through the trees, falling on the ground a short way from the fire.

"What is it?" Damon knelt beside her, placing a protective hand on her back.

Wynne was breathing too hard to speak at first, but

finally she managed to spit out one word: "Bear!" And as she said it a bellowing roar announced the creature's arrival.

The huddled group were leaping to their feet and screaming, backing away from the fire, staring with horror over Damon's shoulder. He turned swiftly, trying to stifle his fear with fake bravery. But the sight of the giant bear, rearing on two legs, its great front paws slashing at the air menacingly, its drooling mouth snapping on invisible flesh, quickly revealed his terror.

The bear dropped onto all fours, eyes boring through Damon as it lumbered towards him.

CHAPTER TWENTY

1

"Damon, back away," cried Wynne, climbing to her feet, her eyes also fixed on the approaching beast. It was three times the size of any bear Damon had ever seen in a zoo, its coat thick and long, matted with dirt and dried blood. One of its front paws could have crushed Damon and Wynne like bugs, one snap of its massive jaws could have bitten either of them clean in two. All this rushed through Damon's mind as he watched the bear and felt the ground tremor with its weight.

"Damon!"

And then he remembered Ariadne's lollipop, still clutched in his hand, glowing faintly after its last magic blast. He raised it, pointing the sticky red disk at the bear, whose hot, stinking breath swamped him as it came within a few feet of where he stood.

"How did you get hold of that?" asked Wynne, her attention switching instantly from the deadly animal to the lollipop.

Damon glared at her. "Does it matter?"

His attention was distracted for just a second, but in that time the bear launched its attack, raising one huge paw and slashing through Damon's jumper with claws like carving knives. Damon screamed, falling backwards, clutching at his stomach. In a confused blur he saw the small wooden chest drop to the ground and a mass of yellow paper explode from his middle, some of it drifting onto the fire, turning black and drifting upwards with the smoke.

He saw Wynne lean over him, grab the lollipop and turn to face the bear, now looming over them both, tearing at the air in front of its ferocious face.

"Get back!" yelled Wynne, tiny against the gigantic bulk of the bear. "Get back!"

The lollipop remained glowing uselessly in her quaking hand. Damon shook himself out of his stupor and stood, checking to see that he hadn't been harmed by the bear's onslaught. The chest and the spell book had saved him.

"Give it to me." He tried to take the lollipop from Wynne but she pushed him away, making him stumble and fall, just inches from the fire. The bear gave a rattling roar and lunged at Wynne, but just as the animal's gaping mouth closed in on her head she thrust out the lollipop and screamed again: "Get back!" And this time a bolt of magic leapt forth, hitting the bear between its bloodshot eyes. The beast staggered backwards, its roar rising in pitch like a scream. Wynne moved forwards, still brandishing the lollipop like a sword: "Back!" she shouted again, her usually gentle voice swollen with anger, and a second bolt, bigger and brighter than the first, shot from the lollipop, slicing through the still reeling bear's left shoulder. Damon saw a chunk of flesh and fur fly from the wild beast, as it twisted round, falling onto all fours and crashed back into the forest.

Wynne took several steps forward as if to give chase to the wounded animal, her face fixed in an expression of rage.

"Wynne?" Damon placed a hand on her shoulder and the expression dissolved. She looked at him, confused, then in the direction that the bear had disappeared. "Did I do that?" she asked.

"Yep!" said Damon.

Wynne sank to the ground, still gripping the lollipop.

"Are you okay?" Damon sat with her, as the others began to gather round, talking excitedly.

"I just feel strange," said Wynne.

Samantha and the rest of the firewood party appeared at the edge of the clearing, all carrying bundles of branches. "What's happened?" asked Samantha. "We heard an animal of some kind. Are you all right Wynne? We lost you. What happened?"

"Let' s get the fire going first," said Wynne. "Just in case it comes back."

"I don't think it will," said Damon, glancing with concern into Wynne's haunted eyes.

George looked very pale for hours after the bear's attack. When Wynne woke in the early hours of the next morning, meagre light beginning to fill the clearing, he was sitting a little way from the fire, rocking backwards and forwards, muttering to himself. She crawled over to where he sat, missing the warmth of the fire. George seemed oblivious to the cold.

"It's gone now, George," Wynne said softly.

He looked at her with bleary, magnified eyes. "Do you think it was the same one?" he asked.

"I don't know," she replied. "It was certainly very big."

George nodded. "I think it was the same one."

Wynne put an arm around his shoulder. "I'm sorry."

"Cinderella!"

The pair looked back to the mass of sleeping bodies. Prince Charming was stepping between them, squinting at each in turn, trying to find his new love.

"She's gone!" he looked imploringly at Wynne and George, as if they held the secret to her disappearance.

"She was there ten minutes ago," said Wynne, I heard her moaning about mice and pumpkins."

"She wouldn't just wander off," said the mystified prince, "Not after that incident with the bear. She hates bears. At least I assume she hates bears."

"Maybe she needed to, you know, do something private," suggested George.

The prince frowned and continued to step round and over the sleeping children. Samantha sat up appearing like a bright buoy amongst the sea of dully dressed children. She pulled up the hood of her dazzling cape and stretched her sleek white fingers to the morning sky. "Morning!" she called breezily.

The Prince was at her side in an instant. "Have you seen her?"

"Who?" asked Samantha, yawning.

"Cinderella. My beautiful, spirited Cinderella?"

"No, not since last night," replied Samantha. "She looked the same as ever – bedraggled and miserable."

The prince tutted loudly and headed towards the edge of the clearing. Samantha watched him go, smiling innocently.

"Careful!" called Wynne, and as she watched him something very odd happened. He disappeared. It wasn't that he'd ducked behind a tree, or fallen suddenly in long grass, he just disappeared completely and then reappeared a second later, still mourning the loss of his love.

Samantha had seen the bizarre incident, too. Her complexion drained of its usual blush and she stood shakily, pointing at the prince as he pushed through the foliage of the forest and disappeared in a more normal fashion.

"What happened then?" she asked. "Did you see that?"

Wynne nodded, not sure how to comfort the disturbed girl.

When the prince returned an hour later he was

distant, sitting apart from the others who were eating small portions of fruit, which Samantha had been carrying in her basket.

"No luck?" asked Wynne, offering him a handful of berries, which he declined with a sharp shake of his handsome head.

"No sign of her," he said. "She's completely disappeared."

"Maybe we should form a search party," suggested Samantha, appearing beside Wynne, her lips stained red with berry juice, brilliant against her plaster-white face.

"There's no point," said the Prince, looking up with moist eyes. "I know what's happening. She's not here any more, she doesn't exist at all. I can feel it. It's like half of me has died. I think we were two halves of the same story. I don't think I can exist without her." The Prince suddenly flickered like the flame of a candle caught in a draught. "I think we were just figments of Ariadne's imagination. She told us that once, said she'd created us to amuse her and that

191

she could extinguish us with a snap of her fingers. We didn't believe her, but I think she was telling the truth. Now that we've escaped, I think we're all going to fizzle out. I think that's what's happened to my Cinderella."

"Don't be ridiculous!" snapped Samantha. "I'm not a figment of anyone's imagination. I'm real, as real as Wynne here!" She prodded Wynne's shoulder painfully as she spoke. "I can remember my life before that mad woman brought me here. I had parents and a grandmother. I was dating a local man...."

"A wood chopper?" suggested Wynne.

"How do you know that?" demanded Samantha. "I haven't told you about him."

"It's all in the story," said Wynne, apologetically.

"I'm real!" insisted Samantha, turning to the Prince to demand some support for her claim, but he had gone. Completely disappeared.

Samantha screamed a long, loud terrified scream and ran into the forest.

CHAPTER TWENTY-ONE

1

When Samantha returned half an hour later looking her usual cheerful self, Wynne decided not to raise the subject of the disappearing Prince and Cinderella. Instead she commented on the bundle of fur the red-caped girl was cradling in her arms along with her basket.

"There's exactly thirty-four of them!" she exclaimed. "All lined up just over there. Thirty-four little fur coats, probably made from that bear you wounded earlier.

Samantha handed one of the coats to Wynne, who examined the rough stitches and hasty workmanship inquisitively. "It's been sewn together with pieces of grass or something similar," she said. "Not very strong, but better than nothing."

The other children gathered round, eagerly selecting a coat that best suited their build. Samantha pointed out the spot where the rest of the garments were lying and the remaining children ran excitedly to find them.

"Whoever made them obviously realised I was warm enough," said Samantha, brushing a wet leaf from her cape. "I don't really feel the cold."

Damon went to say something about fictional characters and the elements, but Wynne trod on his foot and he yelped and refrained from voicing his opinion.

"Who would have done this?" mused Wynne, taking her own coat from Molly, who was already kitted out in fashionable bear fur.

"The shoemaker's elves?" suggested Damon, and Wynne trod on his foot again.

"Is that supposed to mean something to me?" asked Samantha.

"It's a fairy tale, like you," said Damon.

"Well what about you then?" Samantha pointed at Damon, who scowled. "You just appeared out of nowhere the same as me, from what Wynne's told me. How do you know you're real and not just a figment of some witch's imagination?"

"Shut up!" snarled Damon. "I know I'm real."

"Do you?" said Samantha with a sneer. "I think I'm real, but you two aren't convinced. How do you know your past isn't just something you've been created to remember?"

"You could just be part of one of mother's spells," suggested Wynne, looking almost convinced of Damon's fictitious status.

"Oh, grow up!" Damon turned and stomped away.

Samantha smiled smugly. "I can't think why anyone would want to imagine him."

2

When George announced that it was around eight in the morning – he could tell by the position of the sun – they set off for Misty Well; George once again taking the lead with Wynne and Damon.

"What happened to your glasses?" Wynne asked their guide, noticing the bridge was fastened together with a dirty piece of material – probably part of a used handkerchief.

"I'm not sure," said George, "I took them off to wash my face in that stream near to where we camped and when I went to put them back on they were broken in half."

"How long will it take to get to this place?" Damon asked, with a nasty grin.

"At least the rest of the day," said George. "That's if we don't come across any more bears."

"I wasn't asking you," said Damon.

"George knows more than me," said Wynne.

"Oh does he?" Damon quickened his pace so that he was walking ahead of the others.

"Ignore him," Wynne told George.

"He doesn't like me, does he?" George shivered and rubbed his arms through the thin cotton of his shirt.

"Why don't you put your coat on?" suggested Wynne.

George glanced at the ragged fur, which he was

trailing along the ground behind him.

"It doesn't feel right," he said. "Not if it was the bear that killed my parents."

"What could be more right?" said Wynne. "The bear is dead and you get to wear its skin like a trophy."

"I hadn't thought of it like that." After a moment's conjecture, George pulled on the coat.

Behind them Molly piped up: "I need to wee."

"You went five minutes ago," said Joe gently, letting go of her hand.

"I need to go again." Molly was already tottering off to find a private spot.

"Don't go far!" called Joe, as the small girl disappeared behind a clump of bushes.

Molly was feeling tired and fed up with traipsing through woods. At first, freedom from the Pentagram School had made her steps feel so light, she hadn't noticed how much her feet ached or how cold she was. Now, even the thick, but grimy fur coat, was little comfort. She walked a

197

little further from the others, hidden from them by the bushes. She remembered a time before the Pentagram School. It was a very misty memory because she had been just three years old when her desperate mother had left her on the doorstep, but she treasured it nonetheless. The most vivid recollection she had of her childhood – before Ariadne had taken her in her powdered arms and said gleefully: "You pretty little thing. How lovely it will be to watch you play!" – was of a birthday party. Her mother had invited several children from the village over to their small house for tea. Molly remembered all the children seemed a little nervous, as if they didn't get out very much. The Pink Witch often rode through the village on her way to the city so parents tended to discourage their children from wandering the streets. One poor boy who had ventured out alone one day had been blasted twenty feet into the air by a bolt of the evil Pink One's magic. He had lain in bed for weeks, his once black hair white, jabbering madly.

But the birthday party was a happy memory, partly

because of the lovely food – jelly and cakes mainly – and the happy faces of the other children, but mostly because of the clown that had come to entertain everyone. His name had been Ralph and he had been the kindest and funniest man ever!

When Molly saw a clown waving to her from behind a tree, his permanent smile bright and eager in the dimness of the forest, she felt a burst of excitement and happiness bigger than any she had ever felt. She stood and stared at the grinning face and the waving white gloved hand for a few seconds, before running over to their owner.

"Are you Ralph?" she asked, inspecting the painted face more carefully.

"Nope!" said the grinning mouth, and another clown appeared from behind him, causing Molly to squeal.

Both clowns wore big bushy wigs, one red, the other green. Their clothes were ludicrously baggy and their shoes appallingly large. As Molly stared up into their faces she saw that they weren't smiling at all. Both had miserable faces, their mouths small and down-turned, their eyes black and cruel beneath the arched eyebrows.

She was about to make some excuse and run back to the others when two gloved hands grabbed her from behind. One slapped around her mouth to silence her screams, while the second lifted her into the air by the back of her dress. The other two clowns produced a large sack from behind the tree and held it open while the third, whose hair was yellow, threw Molly into it head first. Before she could utter a sound the sack was pulled shut with a length of cord and the three clowns ran off through the trees, all three smiling for the first time that month.

"Molly!" Joe had emerged from the clump of bushes just in time to see the final part of the kidnapping. He tried to give chase, but fell over something partially hidden amongst leaves on the ground. "Molly!"

Wynne and Damon were soon at his side, helping him to his feet.

"What happened?" asked Wynne, as more children

joined them. "Where's Molly?"

"There were clowns," replied a shocked Joe. "Three clowns and they put Molly in a sack."

Damon scowled. "Have you eaten too many of those berries?"

"What's this?" George was crouched, studying the object that Joe had tripped over. He picked it up and handed it to Wynne.

"It's a crystal ball," she said, shuffling the tennis ball-sized orb from one hand to the other.

Suddenly it glowed bright and its misty interior cleared, revealing the panic-stricken face of Molly, cheeks stained with earth liquefied by tears. "Help me!" she screamed, tiny fists rubbing her eyes. And then the ball filled with the leering, lurid face of a clown, its false grin a mass of yellow, jagged teeth.

"The circus is in town!" he called, and as the mist returned and destroyed the image, the forest was filled with his diabolical laughter.

CHAPTER TWENTY-TWO

1

Joe and Cameron had to be restrained from giving chase to the revolting clowns immediately.

"We need to plan this properly," said Wynne when the two boys had calmed down. Damon was sitting with his back to the tree behind which Molly had seen the first clown. He was pretending not to be concerned, but kept thinking of Molly's attempts to befriend him and feeling tearful. There was no way he was going to let himself cry.

"I think the best idea would be to form a small group to go and rescue her," suggested Wynne. "Damon, do you want to come?"

Damon shrugged. "I suppose so."

"I'm coming!" said Joe and Cameron together.

"And me!" piped up George from amongst the gathered children.

"I'll carry on towards Misty Well with the rest,"

202

offered Samantha.

Wynne nodded. That's probably a good idea. And George, I think you should go on to Misty Well too. Your sense of direction could make all the difference. When you get there, explain to Belinda the Beautiful what's happened. Warn her that the Pink Witch may come looking for us. Although I can't imagine the Pink Witch would want to get anywhere near a village full of children."

"No problem," agreed George, his chubby body swelling with pride.

"Don't worry, I'll take care of everything," said Samantha, watching George deflate a little with a faint smile.

"You should be there before it starts to get dark if you start off now," said Wynne, wiping dirt from her pale, tired face with the sleeve of her coat.

"Come on then!" Samantha began to march ahead, beckoning the other children to follow, which after a bemused period of hesitation, they did.

"Heeshee said something about a circus," said Wynne, as they walked through the forest in the direction taken by the clowns. "And I remember hearing people talking about a circus once in our village. They were in the butcher's shop and Mr Bold the butcher was leaning across the counter – his apron was covered in blood, I remember. He was telling two old women about this horrible circus that performed to an audience of children who were forced to clap at every act. When Mr Bold saw me he blushed and started chatting all cheerfully about something else, and the old women both laughed nervously and left."

"Sounds almost as horrible as living with Ariadne the Awful," said Joe. "I wish you'd let me run after them straight away. What was the point in waiting? Now we don't know which way to go."

"A circus shouldn't be too difficult to spot, should it!" said Damon with a scowl.

"There is such a thing as magic around here,"

pointed out Joe, his normally mild manner spiked with aggression. "Spells that disguise things. We could already have walked straight past a circus and thought it was just a few trees standing in a clearing."

"Really?" Damon was genuinely impressed.

"It's not disguised."

The four children spun round to face the owner of the deep, earthy voice.

"You!" Damon exclaimed on seeing the strange nature-loving man he had met the day before, His hairy face was as dirty as ever, strewn with leaves and creeping bugs.

"It's not disguised," repeated the man, as the children stared at him with a mixture of awe and distaste. "It's underground."

"Who are you?" demanded Wynne.

"He's a mad bloke that lives in the forest and feeds on the beauty of nature, or something," explained Damon. "I met him the other day, but he ran off when your mother turned up."

"Not fond of witches," mumbled the man. "Not fond of evil clowns either, but I followed them after they took the little girl. I saw them disappear into a secret entrance not far from here. I can show you if you like."

"Where is it?" Cameron had taken the man by the arm, despite his natural instinct not to touch anything so filthy.

"Don't!" The man shook his arm free. "If you want my help, don't put pressure on me. I can't cope with people who expect too much. That's why I'm here, away from people."

"Just show us, please," begged Joe.

"Yes, take us to the entrance. That's all we want," Wynne reassured the man.

"Are your coats warm?" the man asked as he led the way.

"Did you make them?" asked Wynne, staring up into the man's dark eyes. He nodded and looked away, as if the sight of her embarrassed him.

"Thank you." Wynne considered giving the man's arm a friendly squeeze, but seeing that the arm nearest to her was home to a small nest of earwigs, decided just to smile kindly.

The man scrambled through a particularly dense clump of bushes, the branches of which scratched and tore at the children's clothes and skin. He stopped in the midst of the painful thicket, his mossy clothing almost indistinguishable from the foliage that engulfed him, and bent down. After much grunting and wheezing he stood, holding what appeared to be a square piece of earth in his hands, with a small clump of shrubbery attached to it. On closer inspection Damon saw that it was a trap door, cleverly disguised with greenery and dirt.

"They went this way," said the man, glumly indicating with a nod of his shaggy head into the dark hole he had uncovered.

Damon and the others pushed their way through the prickly bushes to the entrance and looked down. They could just make out a stone step, the second was already lost in darkness.

"Are you going to go after them?" the man looked at Wynne with dark, sad eyes.

"Of course we are," she replied defiantly. "Are you going to help us?"

The man shook his head. "Can't stand it underground. But I'll wait here for you to make sure you come back."

"And what if we don't?" demanded Damon. "What if the mad clowns get us too, what then?"

The man shrugged and looked even sadder. "On second thoughts I'd better go." he said dismally. "Good luck."

He crashed through the bushes, stumbling in his great hurry to be away from the dark hole in the ground.

"Who's going first?" asked Cameron, his eyes wide with apprehension.

"I will if you want," offered Joe.

"Are you sure?" Wynne flashed him an admiring glance.

"I'll go first," said Damon. "We'll be here all day while these two try to decide which one's the biggest hero."

And despite feeling terrified of what lay beyond the entrance, Damon twisted round and began to descend the steps as if they were a ladder. There was no way he was going to let Joe act the hero.

"Careful!" called Wynne, and Damon smiled and felt hot with pride.

At the bottom of the stairs Damon found himself standing in a narrow almost pitch-dark passage. The stone steps were built into one end, so there was only one way to go and it was impossible to see where it led. Cameron joined him a few seconds later, grunting as he jumped down the last few steps, he was soon followed by Joe and Wynne. Wanting to continue in his new role as leader, Damon began to feel his way down the passage. The walls and floor were a damp mixture of earth and crumbling stone. Several times Damon

209

nearly slipped, but in the dark, he hoped this went unnoticed.

"This is impossible," he uttered finally, turning and trying to make out his companions in the blackness. "Wynne, give me the lolly."

"Why?" Wynne sounded suspicious.

"I want to see if I can get it to light up."

"You'll fry us all down here," objected Cameron.

"Just give it to me," insisted Damon.

He heard Wynne tut and rummage inside her coat and then a small gasp. "It's gone!"

"You're joking!"

"No! I had it earlier, I'm sure, but it's not there now. I didn't drop it. I would have noticed that."

"Great!" Damon began to stomp ahead, as much as he could stomp in a pitch-dark underground tunnel. He opened his mouth to shout something about being too young to look after something so important, but a clammy hand slapped across his mouth and pulled him tightly against a solid, cold torso.

"Shhhhhhhhhhhh!" hissed an icy voice that made his skin creep.

CHAPTER TWENTY-THREE

1

The stranger pulled Damon into a small alcove at a point where the tunnel turned right. The hand that covered his mouth smelt musty, like clothes that have been left damp too long, or a dog's coat after it has been in the rain. The skin felt hard and rough, damp and earth-encrusted. And the breath that billowed around Damon's head stank like a fridge that had been left full of rotten vegetables for months.

Damon heard Wynne, Cameron and Joe approach and pass by where he and his captor stood. He was torn between trying to alert Wynne to his presence and letting her pass out of danger. He decided it was best to let her and the others pass. Such an unselfish thought felt strange, but not unpleasant.

When the voices of the other three children had faded, and Damon's heart had sunk as low as it could possibly sink, the hand slipped from his mouth and the stranger hissed in his ear. "That was ssssensible."

"Who are you?" demanded Damon, twisting his neck to look into the man's face. In the darkness all he could make out was a silvery complexion and two beady eyes. The smell of rotting vegetables was overpowering.

"Come on!" hissed the man, yanking Damon further into the alcove.

Damon realised that the darkness of the alcove hid a hole, not much higher than his head, judging from the way his hair brushed the top of the entrance, bringing down a shower of earth and grit. He closed his eyes, crouching so as to avoid another downpour.

"Hurry!" came the icy voice of the stranger, as he dragged Damon through a narrow tunnel that made the original passageway seem spacious. Damon's shoulders rubbed painfully on either side as he stumbled backwards, unable to lift his arm to steady himself, completely in the power of the hissing man.

Suddenly they turned a bend and the tunnel became

even narrower and lower. Damon was forced to sit and allow himself to be hauled along on his back, grimacing against the agony.

"Please!" he called weakly.

"Shhhhhhhhhhhhh!" came the angry response, as they turned another corner, and another.

"Please stop!" yelled Damon, feeling the material at the back of his trousers tear, feeling sharp stones cut at the soft flesh at the top of his legs. Eventually, the tunnel widened and the pair emerged into a small cavern. Damon was flung onto a pile of soft moss, where he lay breathing heavily, trying to block out the searing pain inflicted during the rapid journey through the tunnels.

The cavern was lit by a strange silvery light, which came from a series of glowing orbs positioned at short intervals around the earthy walls.

"Who are you?" he asked the stranger again, turning to get his first clear view of him. But what he saw was not a man. It wasn't a woman either. It was a squirming, grey length of segmented muscle curled just feet away from him like a great rat's tail. The top of the tail-thing widened like a man's torso, the head was shaped almost like a human head, but the features were flat, like those of a man wearing a stocking over his head. From the torso sprouted two human-like arms with large webbed hands and long nails, black with dirt. The thing's mouth was wide and gaping, filled with jagged, rotting teeth, the gaps between them clogged with mud and pulped vegetation. Damon stared, too petrified to even scream. It was as if the creature's hand was still slapped across his mouth.

"Sssstop sssstaring!" hissed the monster. "Here, eat!"

The thing tossed Damon a handful of mashed up moss and what looked like half-digested leaves.

Damon crawled away from the mess, cowering against the wall like an animal about to be shot.

"Eat it!" the monster uncoiled a little, rising up on its powerful tail, like a cobra.

"No!" protested Damon. "I can't eat that! I'd be

sick!"

The creature tilted its head to one side as if in thought.

"Maybe you're right," it mused, and slithered to the opposite side of the cavern, where it curled into a tight ball and fell silent.

"Is it asleep?" wondered Damon, but he dared not move, just in case.

He was right to be cautious, for suddenly, like someone waking from a deep sleep and remembering a hugely important date, the creature propelled itself towards the cave entrance, the muscles in its tail contracting and expanding like springs.

"Don't move!" it hissed, pausing in the doorway. And while Damon watched in horror, the creature opened its mouth and vomited forth a thick white liquid. The liquid turned to a sticky web-like substance in the monster's hands and it weaved a net across the cave entrance, barring any exit from the dank space.

Damon listened to the shuffling, scraping sound of the worm-man moving back along the passages. When the sound had faded, he stood and looked around, trying to find some other means of escape.

He soon discovered that the cave did not end where he had at first thought it did. Standing in the corner where the worm man had seconds ago curled up in thought he found a narrow opening leading to a damp-smelling passageway. He squinted into the darkness, fearful that the tunnel might be populated with more worm men waiting to smother him in sticky liquid and leave him wrapped up like a cocoon. The passage appeared to be deserted, so Damon squeezed through the small gap and began to creep along it.

As his eyes adjusted to the poor light he saw that the walls were made of chalk-like stone, rather than earth and that they were covered in drawings a bit like prehistoric cave paintings. The colours were bright, which meant the drawings were visible even in the semi-darkness. As Damon studied them on his way along the passage he realised they

217

told a story. He retraced his steps back to the entrance and begun to study them more carefully,

The first painting showed a group of worm people, men and women, gathered round a large pile of green stuff, possibly the same strange vegetation the worm man had tried to force him to eat. Several of the group had tendrils of green hanging from their mouth, and the entire clan appeared happy, their crudely drawn faces smiling. One of the male creatures amongst them stood taller than the rest, by at least a foot, and was dressed in a long maroon-coloured cloak, while the others were all naked. The clothed worm man had long grey hair and a beard. He looked, thought Damon, like a typical wizard, apart from the hideous tail protruding from the bottom of his cloak.

Damon edged along, perusing the next tableau. Here the same group were pointing upwards where a bright light was shining. Damon guessed the worm people were supposed to be underground and that the light was the sun shining through a hole. The worm people seemed distressed, their faces etched with round screaming mouths. Only the wizard appeared more angry than scared, as he pointed towards the opening with a long, gnarled staff.

Damon frowned and moved on to the next frame in the story. Now the hole was blocked by a mass of faces, human faces Damon guessed, and several obviously human figures were hanging from the entrance, one dropping amongst the worm people brandishing a lethal looking sword.

"I hope he kills the lot of them!" thought Damon, and in the fourth picture his wish appeared to have been granted. Bloodied bodies, mostly worm people, lay scattered around the pile of green stuff, blank eyes staring towards the hole through which the humans had dropped. In the corner of the picture the wizard was slithering away, his face wracked with pain, with him, clutching his hand, was a much smaller worm man – a child, Damon guessed.

Damon was shocked. He hadn't imagined these things having children. He moved onto the next painting, unnerved by the sight of the worm boy. Here the humans were laughing and dancing around the green stuff, some were eating clumps of it, pushing into their gaping mouths as if their lives depended on it.

Damon felt his stomach churn – nothing could have made him eat that putrid gunk.

In the final picture, just beyond which the passage came to an end, only the wizard and the worm boy were left. The boy was gazing sadly at another pile of the green food. The wizard was far more animated; his arms were spread and a bright yellow bolt of lightning was shooting from his staff into the middle of the heap of vegetation. From the pile rose a misty image of a man, face twisted with agony. Next to this an even fainter image in which the man was no longer a man, but a worm creature, staring at its own tail in horror.

Damon shuddered, and hurried back down the passage, feeling as if he had seen something he was not supposed to have seen and terrified of being caught.

CHAPTER TWENTY-FOUR

1

Damon made it back to the cave just in time. Within seconds of his slumping back in his corner, the worm man appeared outside the makeshift door, clutching something in his right hand. He began to pull at the sticky webbing across the entrance, shoving handfuls of the white mess into his mouth. He guzzled on the webbing until the entrance was entirely clear then threw something on the ground next to Damon who examined it dubiously. It looked like a large apple – a big, red, shiny apple. Damon felt suddenly very hungry. None of the fruit Samantha had collected had looked this appetising.

"Eat it!" insisted the worm man, jabbing a clawed finger at the fruit.

Damon hesitated. Although he didn't like books, he recalled a few stories where people ate apples and ended up in glass coffins or wearing fig leaves and running through gardens.

"What's wrong with it?" he demanded.

"Nothing. Eat it!"

Damon reached out and took the plump fruit in his hand. It felt like an apple. He imagined biting into the red, waxy skin, the crunching sound and the spray of sweet-tasting juice. He was about to give into his desire when he noticed something strange about the apple, other than its size. It had a small hole in it, as if someone had drilled it through to the core. He held the fruit close to his face, squinting into the hole. The worm man watched, shifting from side to side agitatedly. Damon tapped the apple with one finger. It sounded hollow, like a beach ball. Flashing the worm man a suspicious glance, he gripped the giant apple in both hands and with as much force as he could muster, brought it down on a nearby piece of rock. It shattered like china, skin and flesh and juice spraying in every direction. Also spraying in every direction was green sludge, like the concoction the worm man had tried to feed him earlier – the same green stuff that featured in all the pictures in the dark passageway.

The worm man cried out in anger as Damon leapt to his feet shouting: "What is that stuff? Why do you want me to eat the muck so much?"

Damon thought of the pictures again, visualising each in turn, retelling the strange story in his head. Although Damon had never shown himself to be particularly good at understanding anything before, particularly anything other people wanted him to understand, he suddenly understood the tale being told in the primitive-looking drawings.

"It's cursed, isn't it?" he looked into the worm man's weird, silver eyes. "This green stuff is cursed. That old worm man cursed it after the humans tried to steal it. What would have happened to me if I'd eaten it?"

The worm man shrugged, scowling like a child that has been deprived of its favourite toy.

Damon ran back into the narrow passageway, past the first four pictures until he stood facing the last. He stared at the image rising from the pile of green stuff – the ghost-like image of a man, and next to it a similarly feint image of a worm man. Again Damon experienced a rare flash of understanding.

"The man is changing into a thing like you," he whispered. Looking in horror at the worm man who was slithering towards him along the passageway. "The old worm man cursed it so that if any human tried to eat it they would become like you. That's what you were trying to do to me, change me into a monster."

"I am not a monster," hissed the worm man, but as he uttered the words he looked more like a monster than ever, his ghoulish face half in darkness, half lit by the sickly yellow light of the cave, his silver eyes blazing with anger, his jagged teeth bared. "I am not a monster!"

Damon cringed, waiting for the creature to attack, but instead he saw the strangest thing – large glistening tears were rolling down the worm man's flat face.

"Are you crying?" Damon asked, incredulously.

"No!" insisted the worm man, turning away and slithering back towards the cave.

Damon hesitated and then ran after him.

"I'm right aren't I? The green stuff is cursed."

Damon wondered if he had always been this bright and just never bothered to use it before.

"Yes, you're right," snarled the worm man, flopping in the corner of the cave in which he had originally pushed Damon.

"And you tried to feed it to me. Why would you want me to be like you?"

The worm man was silent, his face hidden under a scaly arm.

"Well?" insisted Damon, stamping his foot in a manner that reminded him of his old self.

"Company!" yelled the worm man looking up with eyes blurred by tears. "I wanted some company."

Damon stared, completely taken aback by the reply. "I don't understand."

The worm man sat up, wiping tears from his face and sniffing loudly. "How old do you think I am?" he asked.

Damon shrugged, again completely unprepared for the question.

"I'm thirteen," said the worm man. "About the same age as you, probably. I'm thirteen and there is no-one else like me alive, not anywhere around here anyway. The last one of my people died two years ago – the elder that you saw in the cave pictures. He drew those before he died. And yes he did curse the green stuff."

Damon noticed that the worm man, or worm boy as he turned out to be, was not hissing so much anymore. Perhaps that had been for effect to make himself seem more threatening.

"Why did the humans want the green stuff anyway?" asked Damon.

"Because it keeps them young," said the worm boy between sniffs. "At least that's what they thought. For us it was a major source of nourishment. It's a kind of moss that only grows in underground caves. We used to harvest it in the old days. Then the humans came and gorged themselves on it, killing all my people except me and the elder who brought me here to safety."

Damon was lost for words. The old Damon would have stormed from the cave and left the strange creature to cry, but his story had touched the new Damon.

"I'm sorry for what the humans did," he said. "But I wouldn't be happy living here underground. I would make a terrible friend because I would always hate you for turning me into…"

"A monster?" offered the worm boy bitterly.

"I have my own friends who I need to get back to," continued Damon.

"The ones I saw you with?" asked the worm boy.

"Yes – Wynne, Joe and Cameron – they're looking for a little girl called Molly who was kidnapped by evil clowns."

"From the Circus of Lost Souls?"

"You know about it?" Damon took a step towards him.

"Of course I know about it. I hear the music sometimes – awful, dreary music that crawls into your head and twists up your brain."

"Can you show me where it is?" asked Damon.

The worm boy laughed humourlessly. "Why would I want to do that?"

"To make up for trying to feed me cursed moss."

"And what are you going to do to make up for killing all my family and friends?"

"I didn't kill them."

"Your people did."

"Not my people. I don't even come from this world. I've only been here a few days. Nothing that happens here is anything to do with me."

The worm boy cocked his head to one side. "You come from another world?"

"Yes. A much nicer world than this, where there are no witches and no evil rituals and no…"

"Monsters like me?"

"Stop putting words into my mouth!" snapped Damon.

"You put them there yourself not so long ago."

"I didn't know you then."

"You don't know me now."

"You know what I mean. Anyway, can I go now? I'm not going to eat that stuff and even if you forced me you couldn't keep me here forever so you'd end up on your own again eventually."

"My people came from another world," said the worm boy, ignoring Damon. "Hundreds of years ago my ancestors came here from another world populated by millions like me. They were running away because they had committed a crime and were going to be executed, but if I could find my way there…How did you get here?"

"A funny little fat man brought me."

The worm boy frowned. "What fat man?"

"I don't know who he was. He told me I could either die a hideously painful death in a fire or come here. So I came here."

"Would you know where to find him again?"

"Wouldn't have a clue," admitted Damon. "I was hoping he would just turn up at some point and take me back. I've been too busy to think about it, what with rescuing kids from evil witches and trying to get them to Misty Well..."

"Misty Well!" ejected the worm boy. "Misty Well where Belinda the Beautiful lives?"

"Yes," said Damon, frowning.

"I've tried to find that place before. There's a mystic well there that some believe was once used as a gateway to other worlds."

"Really?" Damon was as excited at this news as his new companion.

The worm boy curled up in the corner again, deep in thought. When he uncoiled, his face bore a decisive expression. "I'll help you find your friends if you take me with you to Misty Well."

"What?" Damon was not drawn to this plan.

"It's the only way I'll ever be amongst my own kind again," said the worm boy.

"I think I'll just take my chances, " said Damon, taking a step towards the cave entrance.

The worm boy let out a blood-curdling hiss and rose up on his muscular tail, quivering like a snake about to strike with lethal fangs.

"There again," said Damon hastily. "I could do with some company."

CHAPTER TWENTY-FIVE

1

Damon followed the worm boy through a maze of musty-smelling tunnels. Some were dry and dusty, each breath of air bringing with it a tickling smog that clogged up Damon's nostrils and made his throat sore; other tunnels were damp, the low ceilings dripping water that smelt like sweat.

The worm boy's name, Damon had discovered, was Kiskis. When Kiskis pronounced the name himself it lasted for about 10 seconds, the last 's' trailing off into a long hiss. His people were not called worm men and women, but were known as Mosstrols.

He gave Damon a brief account of his life as they made their way towards the Circus of Lost Souls. The last two years had been spent almost entirely in the pokey cave. Because the precious moss that held all the nutrients Mosstrols needed to live a healthy life, was becoming increasingly difficult to find, he was forced to feed on small animals and birds' eggs which he scavenged for at night.

"I generally avoid your kind," he explained. "Humans tell their children horror stories about Mosstrols to keep them in their beds at night."

"What is the Circus like?" Damon blurted, suddenly unable to hide his apprehension.

Kiskis stopped and looked back, his silver face eerie in the darkness.

"Letsss just sssay you wouldn't choose to visit," he said, the hiss more pronounced then ever, as if enhanced by his nerves.

"What's so awful about it?"

"You'll sssoon see."

And as Kiskis spoke a horrible, squirmingly nasty music snaked its way along the tunnel. It was like the worst tune you could possibly imagine, played on an instrument that could have been a violin, but a violin that had never been tuned and by someone who had never been taught how to play it.

Damon grimaced.

"The show's sssstarted," hissed Kiskis.

Soon Damon saw a dull light ahead, with Kiskis framed in the tunnel mouth. For a second he looked like one of the drawings from the cave wall that told the tragic story of his people. Damon shuffled the final few feet of the tunnel and stood just behind him, peering over a scaly shoulder.

"Wow!" he gasped.

The tunnel mouth was set hundreds of feet up in the side of an immense cavern. Damon saw other tunnel entrances dotted across the grey/green walls. And way below, spread across the cavern floor was the biggest tent Damon had ever seen, striped every possible colour, but dulled by years of falling earth and flaking rock. It looked, thought Damon, like a giant version of a child's tent that had been left too long in the back garden.

The hideous music rose up, curdling the contents of Damon's stomach.

"How do we get down there?" he asked, part of him hoping it would be impossible.

"The quickest way would be to jump," said Kiskis, staring bleakly at the big top. "But the fabric of that thing is so old and rotten we would probably fall right through it."

"How then?" asked Damon, relieved that plan A had already been shelved.

Kiskis didn't answer. He opened his mouth and without warning began to vomit up the same sticky mess he had used to seal the entrance to his cave.

Damon stepped back, scowling.

But Kiskis kept spewing forth the web-like material. It dangled like a thick thread from his gaping mouth, falling like a rope towards the big top.

Damon realised that plan B was going to be just as unpleasant as plan A.

Ten minutes later Kiskis was tying the end of the long tendril of spewed silky substance to a rock just inside the tunnel entrance. He spewed a little more of the sticky stuff around the rock to ensure the vomited rope was securely fastened then turned to Damon.

"There," he said, silver eyes twinkling. "Now we don't have to jump."

"Great," said Damon.

"I'll go first," said Kiskis, dropping over the edge of the tunnel mouth.

Damon gasped and looked down. Kiskis was negotiating his way expertly down the makeshift rope, his long, muscular tail entwined around it like a coiled snake.

"Come on!" he called, already half way down.

Damon felt dizzy just looking down to the floor of the great cavern. The thought of stepping over the edge, of dangling hundreds of feet from the ground on a piece of rope that had come from something's mouth filled him with dread.

"I can't!" he shouted back, stepping away from the edge and placing a hand on the nearest wall to steady himself.

"You managed to drop from the window of the tower at the Pentagram school," he told himself. "If you can do that you can do this. If you fall maybe the flying feeling will come back and you'll float down slowly like a feather."

But what if he fell and the flying feeling didn't come back? What if he dropped like a stone, hitting the ground at a hundred miles per hour?

He began to shake violently.

"Hurry!" he heard Kiskis call.

"I can't do it!" he shouted angrily.

"Of course you can!" a voice spoke inside his head, and it wasn't his own voice. "Here you can do anything you put your mind to. I didn't go to all this trouble for you to stay stuck in a musty little tunnel for the rest of your life."

It was the voice of the funny little man that had brought him to Lightsleep.

"It's easy for you to say," said Damon, "you're not scared of heights!"

But the little man's voice did not come again.

Damon took a deep breath and stepped towards the tunnel mouth. Without looking down he turned and knelt with his back to the light, gripping the end of the sticky rope where it met the rock around which Kiskis had tied it.

"You have to do this," he whispered. "You have to find Wynne and the others. You have to help save Molly."

He took several more deep breaths then shuffled on his knees until his feet and ankles were hanging over the edge of the tunnel opening.

"One…"

He edged a little further back until his knees were rocking on the edge.

"Two…."

He lay flat against the tunnel floor and shuffled back further, his legs stiff like those of an action figure that had no bend in its knees.

"Three!"

Gripping the rope like a much-loved possession he dropped over the edge, yelping fearfully as his toes bumped against the cavern wall.

He hung there for a few seconds, eyes screwed shut, his entire body rigid, and then began to slowly, nervously shin down the rope.

What seemed like hours later, but was in fact only a few minutes, he reached the ground.

"I was about to have a sleep," said Kiskis, as Damon let out a relieved sigh and opened his eyes.

Kiskis did indeed look as if he had been considering a nap, coiled amongst a pile of rocks, arms folded, the end of his tail propped on one large stone as if it were a leather foot rest, like the one Damon's grandparents owned.

Just feet away, close enough to touch, was the grimy, red canvas-like wall of the huge tent. And Damon was suddenly aware again of the hideous music that trailed from within like the cries of a dying animal.

He was about to ask what they should do next when a hand rested on his shoulder and his insides turned cold.

CHAPTER TWENTY-SIX

1

Damon turned, expecting to see the leering face of a deranged clown, or some other freakish creature from the circus, but instead it was the pale, dirty face of Wynne that stared back at him. Her cheeks were streaked with tears, her hair matted with earth and dust.

"Damon, I'm so glad you're here," she whispered and fainted into his arms.

Kiskis watched on impatiently as Damon sat Wynne gently on the ground with her back to the cavern wall.

"Wynne," he called softly, stroking her head like a caring parent. If he'd paused to think about how nice he was being, Damon would probably have ceased instantly and told Wynne to pull herself together and stop being such a baby, but he didn't think about it. He just saw that Wynne looked vulnerable and pale and wanted to make her better.

"What's wrong with her?" demanded Kiskis.

"How should I know?" said Damon. "I'm not a doctor. Just shut up for a minute."

Eventually Wynne opened her bleary eyes and looked miserably at Damon. "He took them both," she said. "I couldn't stop him. It was terrible."

"Who took them?" asked Damon, glancing around in case the kidnapper was still on the prowl.

"Magento the Magnificent," replied Wynne.

"Who?" Damon's frowned.

"He's some sort of warlock," said Wynne, still dazed.

"Used to be right hand man to King Arold," said Kiskis, casually.

"What?" Damon looked questioningly at the worm boy, who was filing his long fingernails with a flat piece of stone.

"Sorry?" Kiskis glanced up, as if unaware he had spoken.

"What do you know about this Magento the Magnificent?" asked Damon.

"Not much. Just what I've picked up over the years. You hear a lot from up above while you're crawling around looking for scraps of food. I lived underneath the Royal Palace for a few months – the scraps were of a higher quality there. But I got homesick eventually and left the high life behind me."

Wynne stared at Kiskis, noticing him for the first time, She looked back at Damon, eyes wide.

"I think he's safe," said Damon, reading her thoughts. "He did try and feed me cursed leaves at first but he seems to have got over that now."

Wynne did not appear consoled.

"Magento, if it's the same one, was right-hand man to King Arold," continued Kiskis, in a self-important tone. "He used to be known as the real ruler of Lightsleep, because Arold was always too drunk to make any decisions himself. Anyway, Magento went too far, he tried to poison the king

243

having got him to sign over all rights to the throne of Lightsleep to him. The plot failed and Magento was sentenced to death by burning. He escaped. Nobody knew where he had gone. He cropped up here a few years ago – not long after I arrived back myself. I saw him groping his way along the tunnels carrying a huge old carpet on his back. He was muttering like a mad man. He soon discovered the weird circus bunch – they've been here for as long as I can remember, but they were fairly quiet until he came along."

"That's the most he's said since I met him," said Damon to Wynne. "And not one hiss. I think he just does that for effect."

Kiskis hissed aggressively.

Wynne looked at Damon with a mixture of puzzlement and admiration.

"What?" asked Damon.

"You just sounded very grown up," said Wynne.

"Don't be stupid!"

"Were you planning to rescue these friends of yourssss?" asked Kiskis, allowing the final 's' to trail on for a good five seconds.

"Yes!" snapped Damon. "Tell us everything you know about where he's taken them?" Damon placed a hand on each of Wynne's shoulders as if to steady her.

Wynne took a deep breath. "We found our way into this place about an hour ago. We realised you weren't with us and went back a little way to try and find you. When we couldn't, we decided to try and find Molly first and then look for you on the way back."

"Oh, I was being well looked after," said Damon.

"So," continued Wynne, wearily, "we crept around the big top until we found a tear that we could crawl through. Cameron went first, I think, then Joe, then me. We found ourselves crouched behind a row of wooden seats. There were children sitting on all of them. We crawled along a little way until we reached an aisle between the seats. From there we could make out part of the circus ring and see a lot of the audience." Wynne closed her eyes as if feeling dizzy again. "It was awful," she said eventually. All these children staring blankly at the circus ring, their mouths hanging open. They were like zombies – I suppose that's what they are. And then that terrible music started and we saw clowns flashing past the end of the aisle, cart-wheeling and tumbling and the children in the audience started clapping. They clapped slowly and without any feeling. Oh, Damon, it sounded like dead people clapping. It was horrible!"

Over the gut-curdling music, Damon thought he heard the dull sound of dead applause.

"What happened next?" he asked softly.

"Things just got worse," replied Wynne, wiping a tear from her face. "Suddenly we were all grabbed from behind by these bedraggled looking men and women. They were dressed in clothes that had obviously once been bright, glittering circus outfits, but they were so old and dirty all the colour and glitter was hidden. Their hair was grey and covered in dust and cobwebs. They looked like they had crawled out of their graves to get to us."

Wynne paused, taking several long tremulous breathes and then continued: "There were about six or seven of them. They dragged us down the aisle and across the circus ring, where the clowns were still performing. We were thrown behind a large grey curtain and told to lie in silence while one of them went to get Magento the Magnificent. While one man went off, his friends walked round us like wild cats cornering their prey. And then Magento the Magnificent appeared – what a sight! Billowing purple robes that were clean and bright compared to the other circus people' clothes and a great red turban piled high on his fat, round head. His skin was very white, like the others, but his eyes had an evil glint that made him look more alive than his henchmen – and henchwomen. He had a nasty wispy beard that was twisted into two long threads, fastened at the ends with little white beads. He gave us all a look of such complete and utter hatred I though we were all going to die there and then."

"But you didn't," said Damon, trying to inject a positive note into the story.

"I wish we had," wept Wynne. "It would have been better than what actually did happen."

"What?" Damon rubbed Wynne's shoulders, trying to calm her enough so that she could go on.

"We were forced through a series of rooms, all with walls made out of the tent material, all smelling musty and damp, most of them piled high with old chests and broken bits of circus equipment – trapezes, costumes, cages. Eventually, we were thrown onto the floor of a small room that had nothing in it but a small round table. On top of the table was a crystal ball – much bigger than the one the clowns left in the forest. Magento stood in front of it while his evil followers herded us into a corner. Poor Joe looked terrified; even Cameron looked scared.

"Magento gave us another hateful glare and then began to move his hand over the top of the crystal ball and mutter in a deep, ugly voice. I felt the hairs on the back of my neck stand on end and goose pimples break out on my arms. I had to get out of that room, Damon. I had to!"

Wynne began to sob again.

Kiskis hissed impatiently. Damon flung him a chastising look.

"Then what happened?" Damon asked, trying to hide his own impatience.

"Joe screamed. His mouth dropped open and he started to scream. And then…" Wynne's story was broken by further sobs. "And then I saw it fly out of his mouth. It looked like a ghost, a shimmering blue ghost."

"What did?" Damon wondered if Wynne had lost her mind.

"His soul. I think it was his soul. I saw it fly out of his screaming mouth and into the crystal ball. For a second I saw Jo's face peering from the ball, all distorted as if it was a reflection in a hall of mirrors. Then it was gone and Joe was sitting next to me staring straight ahead, Not blinking. Just staring like the children in the circus audience had been staring. It was horrible, but it doesn't excuse what I did."

"What did you do?" asked Damon.

"I ran. I leapt up and shoved past the circus people guarding the entrance to the room. I took them by surprise – they were so enthralled by what their master was doing they'd forgotten to keep an eye on me. They tried to grab me with their grey flaky hands, but I struggled free and bolted. I ran from one room to the next, sometimes I'd disturb other circus people sitting at stained old mirrors, putting on their garish make-up. In one big room there were cages filled with sickly looking lions and tigers. They barely even growled as I ran through. I could hear Magento the Magnificent's henchmen just behind me. I thought they would grab me any second, but I didn't look back. Finally, I ran into a room that had no exit other than the flap through which I'd entered. All there was to escape through was a small tear in the fabric of the tent in the far wall. I was half way through when Magento's helpers burst in. I thought that was it, but I managed to get through just as their dry, powdery hands reached for me. I fell onto the ground and realised I was outside. Magento's people tried to follow but the rip was too small and while they struggled to make it bigger I picked myself up and took off. I found a tunnel like the one that had lead us here and hid just inside. I was there for ages before I saw you. And that's it," concluded Wynne, wiping more tears from her eyes. "That's the end of the story about how Wynne left two friends to the most hideous fate, because she was a complete coward who deserves to die."

Chapter Twenty-seven

1

It took a good twenty minutes to calm the distraught Wynne.

Damon kept telling her that anyone would have done the same thing in her situation – and no doubt he would have done – that she hadn't been a coward at all and what could she have done to save her friends if she'd let Magento the Magnificent do whatever he had done to them to her too?

When her wailing had subsided to gentle sobs, Damon turned to Kiskis, who was still preening himself nonchalantly.

"Any ideas?" he asked.

"About what?" Kiskis looked up, admiring the black nails on his manicured right hand.

"About how to save our friends."

"Why would I want to waste my time thinking about ways of saving your friends?" asked Kiskis.

"Because if you don't, I won't help you find your way home."

Kiskis scowled. "You'll never get them back now. A lot of children end up in that place, but I've never seen one leave. Ever since Magento arrived the circus people have become his slaves. He sends them out hunting for children. I hear them screaming sometimes as they're dragged through the tunnels. It's a horrible sound."

"Didn't stop you doing the same to me though, did it?" said Damon.

"I crept down here once or twice to see if I could grab any of the children for myself, feed them the cursed moss and make them into companions. But as soon as I saw their faces and their endlessly clapping hands, I knew they were useless to me. He steals their souls and forces their mindless bodies to sit and applaud every act – especially hissss."

Kiskis' last 's' lasted for several seconds, his eyes glazed over as he pictured the soulless children.

"That is so horrible," said Wynne, dismally. "And that's what he's done to Cameron and Joe – and I let him!" Tears welled in her eyes.

"Oh don't start again!" snapped Kiskis.

"Yeah, come on Wynne," said Damon. "We have to think about what we're going to do."

It didn't even cross Damon's mind that these were people he wasn't supposed to care about, that Wynne wasn't really his sister and this strange world wasn't anything to do with him.

Wynne nodded and wiped the fresh tears away.

"I do have an idea, actually," said Kiskis.

Wynne and Damon both looked at him expectantly.

"If we were to enter the tent from the top, would you be able to tell when we were above the room with the crystal ball?"

Wynne looked up, imagining the huge expanse of canvas that formed the roof of the big top. "I'm not sure," she admitted. "But I could try."

2

It took the three nearly half an hour to scramble up the dusty, earth-encrusted tarpaulin of the big top. Kiskis made the task of scaling the side easier by spewing forth another of his makeshift ropes, which he expertly hooked over a protruding tent rod some fifty feet above their heads. Eventually, all three were sprawled across the sloping roof of the tent, which spread for hundreds of feet ahead and on both sides of them sweeping up to a point from which a bedraggled, colourless flag hung. There was no breeze to stir it in the depths of the huge cavern.

"Now," said Kiskis. "Where was the room in which Magento kept the crystal ball?"

Wynne bit her bottom lip until it was bloodless, gazing out across the murky sea of tarpaulin. "It was definitely in that direction," she said nodding to their left. "I ran through loads of rooms, but I didn't cross the circus ring once and we were taken off to the left by Magento's henchmen."

"Can you be a little more precise," said Kiskis, using his hiss to sinister effect with the final word.

Wynne blew through her lips and continued to stare across the big top. "I think we only passed through a couple of rooms before we reached the crystal ball."

"You lead the way," suggested Kiskis, his tone betraying a lack of confidence in Wynne's ability to find the right spot.

Damon was feeling dizzy as he tried desperately not to look down. While much about Damon had changed since his arrival in the weird world of Lightsleep, his fear of heights remained. He was glad to crawl after Wynne and Kiskis, away from the edge of the roof. He listened to the eerie music rising up from under them and hoped they were too high above the action of the circus ring to be detected.

"It could have been somewhere around here," said Wynne, as they came to a stop around the centre of the left-hand slope of the big top.

"Let's hope you're right," said Kiskis, and with one of the talons on his right hand he sliced through the rotting material of the tent. Damon shivered, imagining what those claws could have done to him had he and Kiskis not formed their uneasy alliance.

Kiskis pushed his head through the resulting hole, pulling it free seconds later.

"Try again," he hissed angrily. "There's nothing down there but cages filled with sickly animals."

Wynne sat with her knees pulled up to her chest and surveyed the big top once again. "In that case the crystal ball room must be just over there," she said, setting off at a fast crawl, back the way they had come.

Kiskis sighed and followed, Damon, still out of breath from the initial climb onto the roof, trailed a little way behind.

Wynne stopped some thirty feet from the previous spot and pointed downwards. "Try here," she instructed, sounding more like her old self again.

"Yessss ma'am," said Kiskis, pointing at her face with a black razor-sharp nail for a second before plunging it into the tarpaulin and slicing another gash through which to peer. "Well done," he said patronisingly as he drew his head free.

"Is it the right room?" asked Wynne, surprised by her own success.

Kiskis nodded. "And it's empty apart form the table and the crystal ball. Now all we need to decide is which one of you is gong to be lowered down there to get it."

Damon's stomach lurched. He wasn't sure if his nerves would survive another experience of being dangled more than a hundred feet above the ground.

"I'll go," said Wynne. "I'm the lightest and I feel responsible."

"Why do we need it anyway?" asked Damon.

"Isn't it obvious?" spat Kiskis. "We need it so we can destroy it and set the souls of the children free."

"Is that all it will take?" asked Wynne doubtfully.

Kiskis shrugged. "I'm only guessing."

Wynne looked at Damon and smiled faintly. "I suppose it's worth a try," she said.

Damon shrugged. "If we're wrong we could end up trapping them forever. Which in Jo's case might not be such a bad thing."

Wynne's face darkened. "Don't say that."

"Are you going or not?" demanded Kiskis.

Wynne nodded and Kiskis began to vomit forth more of the extremely useful webbing.

CHAPTER TWENTY-EIGHT

1

Damon watched as Wynne slowly shinned down the sticky rope, her face contorted with the effort. He felt guilty for not offering to make the descent himself, but at the same time relieved not to be placed in such danger. He had never felt protective towards anyone before and the feeling felt strangely warm, yet painful.

Wynne looked up at Damon. "You won't let go will you?" she called.

"Oh yes!" snapped Kiskis. "That was the plan."

"Shut up!" snapped Damon, thinking how familiar Kiskis seemed considering he had only known him a short time. He wondered if the worm boy reminded him of someone from his own world.

Wynne frowned and continued to climb downwards, small hands shifting one under the other until she finally reached the ground.

"Hurry!" hissed Kiskis, "Grab the crystal ball and tie the end of the rope around your waist. We'll pull you up."

Wynne nodded, looking tiny so far below.

But as she lay her hands upon the cold, misty globe, a rustling sound alerted her to a new arrival in the room and she turned sharply to see Magento striding towards her, his eyes bright with rage, the long fingers of his right hand stretched towards her, as if to conjure her soul from its shell before she had time to even scream.

"You little thief!" he cried, stopping a few feet from where Wynne stood, still clutching the beach ball-sized orb. "Step away from it, now!"

He sounded, thought Damon, like an actor from an early American film and moved like one from a silent movie – arms gesticulating wildly, expressions exaggerated as if he needed to convey his emotions to a cinema audience watching in the dark. Damon had sometimes watched these old movies with his mother, complaining all the way through that they were boring, but actually enjoying them.

A group of Magento's dusty followers crept up behind him, their black eyes sizing Wynne up malevolently. Two clowns appeared in the entrance, their curly wigs the only colour amongst the group of circus folk. They grinned at Wynne, revealing sharpened fangs.

Wynne fixed her gaze on Magento's furious eyes, refusing to look upwards and betray her friends, although she knew Magento was bound to notice the rope hanging down from the roof sooner or later.

"Time for you to join your fellow trespassers, I think," said Magento wiggling his index finger as he spoke and flicking his head as if to clear a long fringe from his eyes. In fact all his hair was tucked underneath his turban

"Help," whispered Wynne, tears prickling the corners of her eyes.

Magento began to chant, taking a step towards her. Wynne felt her mouth drop open and her face grow stiff. "Please help!" she thought. And as the thought entered her head Magento shrieked and stumbled backwards. Wynne felt her face relax. The self-confessed great magician continued to shriek and spit and caterwaul as his hands grappled with something that had attached itself to his face, covering his eyes.

"It's webbing," said Wynne out loud.

"Come on!" called Damon and Kiskis, and before the circus folk or Magento had time to react, Wynne grabbed the end of the rope with one hand, tucked the crystal ball under her free arm, and shouted: "I'm ready, pull me up!"

Slowly Wynne began to rise. Her feet were dangling just a few feet from the ground as the monochrome circus people began to creep towards her. They were still dangerously low as Magento managed to pull Kiskis's web bomb from his face and clamber to his feet.

"Hurry!" she called, curling her legs up as far as possible.

Grey hands were clutching at her feet, split, earth-stained nails brushing the soles of her shoes.

Magento was glaring up at her, anger mixed with hatred in his blazing eyes.

"Smash it!" came the thin yet forceful voice of Kiskis. "Smash the ball, now!"

Wynne hesitated, remembering Damon's bleak prediction should Kiskis's theory be incorrect.

"Do it!" insisted Kiskis, still high above her.

Wynne glanced at Magento, who was chanting once again, the circus people crouched around him like wild cats surrounding a tree. She felt her face began to stiffen and without giving herself further time to consider the outcome, she threw the crystal ball with all possible force towards the stony ground.

Magento's expression flicked to horror as the ball dropped and shattered, spraying shards of misty glass in every direction.

A terrible wailing filled the tent and ghost-like shapes began to rise from the fragments, swirling like smoke then slipping from the room, either through the cracks around the closed flap of the entrance or the gaps between the walls and the ground. Hundreds of the shapes rose, dancing on the still, stale air before following the others towards the circus ring.

Magento began to shriek madly, waving his arms like an insane conductor. "Come back! Come back!" he called, tears of rage streaming down his hot, red face.

Wynne dropped from the rope and easily ducked past the stunned circus folk, following the last of the stolen souls out of the room and through the maze of rooms beyond until she stumbled into the circus ring.

It was a wonderful sight that met her. Everywhere children were laughing and hugging each other as their souls slipped back into their bodies. Some of the children looked dazed, but their faces were still lit by wide smiles.

Wynne saw Cameron and Joe standing at the edge of the ring, looking around as if for a lost friend. She ran to join them hugging each in turn and repeatedly saying how sorry she was.

"It was horrible," admitted Joe. "Half of me felt as though I was floating – but it wasn't a nice feeling – it was like being on a small boat in really rough water; and then part of me could see the circus ring and that awful man performing tricks and flying backwards and forwards on his magic carpet and however hard I tried I couldn't bring the two halves of me back together again. I just had to keep clapping and floating."

"There's Molly!" announced Cameron, excitedly. Molly, bleary eyes, legs wobbling slightly, tottered across the ring and fell into Jo's arms.

"I still need to go for a wee," she said.

All three older children laughed, but their celebrations had to wait, as slicing through the sound of merriment came the dramatic cries of Magento the Magnificent. He floated to the centre of the ring on a carpet that would have filled an entire room in Damon's house back in the real world. He was standing with both arms raised, as if preparing to call bolts of lightning from the sky.

"You'll all suffer for this!" he bellowed. "I'll find each and every one of you and steal your souls for good this time. One night when you least expect it, I'll float up to your bedroom window and tap on the glass. When you come to see who it is that wants you at such a late hour you'll see my face pressed against the pane and in my right hand I'll be holding another crystal ball – a more powerful, stronger crystal. I'll smile at you through the glass and then you'll hear my chanting and feel your body turn stiff. It will be the last thing your body ever feels because once I have collected each and every soul I will cast the ball into the deepest ocean where no-one will ever find it. Those of you who hear my tapping and dive fearfully beneath their bed covers will only be delaying the inevitable. Soon, from your makeshift cocoon, you will hear my footsteps on the soft carpet then my fingers gripping the edge of your sheets and pulling them back inch by inch so that the chill air blasting through the open window bites into your flesh."

"Oh shut up!" came a familiar voice and every face in the circus ring turned to the main entrance. There stood Damon, hands planted defiantly on his hips, lower jaw jutting aggressively, eyes fixed on the surprised face of Magento.

"What did you say!" demanded the magician, turning on his magic carpet to face the cocky newcomer.

"I said shut up," replied Damon and suddenly he floated into the air until he stood level with Magento.

Magento looked perturbed. He was not used to being challenged. Since he had discovered the underground circus and its dishevelled performers his leadership had never been questioned. The circus folk had been in hiding for years, on the run from the ruler of a distant land for causing the death of his daughter in a badly judged act of audience participation. The ruler's daughter had ended up crushed beneath the foot of a nearsighted elephant and had died three days later. Although the circus had moved on by then, the king had offered huge sums of money for the corpse of any member of the troupe brought to his palace. After days of travelling the troupe had discovered a cave, which led to a tunnel wide enough for their caravans to pass through and eventually to the cavern. The tunnel had long since collapsed and the circus people had settled miserably into their subterranean lifestyle.

When Magento had appeared, with the power to conjure forth food and an audience, they had been more than happy to serve him. Damon's blunt act of insubordination made the magician flinch as if he had been slapped.

Damon was terrified – and also rather shocked that he had managed to levitate himself simply by willing it. He looked perfectly composed, however – Damon had always been good at hiding his true feelings.

"You don't know me," he said pointing at Magento. "But I know you. I am Damonian, spirit of ill-treated children, protector of the abused, and your time is up!"

Magento's jaw dropped. "What…?" he spluttered.

"When I clap my hands," said Damon, "You will fall to the ground and grovel in the dirt. You will beg these children for forgiveness and then you will scurry like a frightened rat into the tunnels and take your motley followers with you. If I ever see you again I will destroy you."

"Don't be ridiculous!" spat Magento.

Damon clapped his hands. Magento toppled from his flying carpet and landed on the ground in an ungainly heap. The children standing behind him had seen the thick strand of sticky webbing drop from a small hole high above them in the big top ceiling. They had watched open-mouthed as it attached itself to Magento's robes and gasped as it was tugged backwards, yanking the magician from his floating platform.

Magento, on the other hand, saw none of this. All he knew was that when Damon had clapped his hands he, a great magician, had fallen, just as the child had said he would. In truth, Magento wasn't that magnificent at all. He could conjure simple objects like food, he could perform the odd trick with a hat and a rabbit and even make a woman float in mid air, if he put his mind to it. But all these tricks had taken him years to master. He relied on magical artefacts for his power – crystal balls to trap the souls of lost children and flying carpets, created by the magic of others far more powerful than him. Therefore, this child who floated in mid-air without the help of any carpet and who could send him falling backwards with one clap, frightened Magento.

He considered his options while he lay in the dirt, surrounded by children. He considered them quickly.

"Well!" bellowed Damon, in a voice he barely recognised as his own.

Magento leapt to his feet and ran through the crowds of children disappearing through a flap of decaying material. A search by a group of children minutes later revealed that the circus folk had followed him, off in search of a new hiding place.

Damon, Wynne, Cameron, Joe and Kiskis led the hundreds of children through the maze of tunnels until finally they emerged into sunlight on what could have been the same day they had entered the underground world or days later –

no-one could say for sure how long the adventure had taken. They found themselves in a vast yellow field surrounded on every side by dense forest.

"We'll have to come back and free the animals some time soon," said Wynne.

Damon nodded. The need to liberate the unfortunate beasts hadn't occurred to him.

"You can leave that to me," said a gruff, earthy voice close by.

Standing a little way from the hole from which the children had emerged – and from which many more were still emerging – was the man from the forest.

"How did you get here?" demanded Wynne.

"I've been wandering round for hours, waiting for you to re-appear," said the man. "There's tunnel entrances all over the woods, and the surrounding fields but something told me you'd come out of this one. I'm not the only one who's been waiting for you either." And from behind the man waddled the familiar figure of Toshi, tutting away to himself as always.

Before Wynne or Damon could squeal his name, Toshi made an announcement.

"You must get to Misty Well immediately," he said.

"The Pink Witch is on her way there now. She's chasing the Talisman of Evil – it was Ariadne's lollipop all the time!"

CHAPTER TWENTY-NINE

1

"How did you find us, Toshi?" asked Wynne.

"I just flew over the woods searching for you," replied the bird. "Eventually I caught sight of this gentleman standing in a clearing looking around him as if he had lost something and I flew down and asked if he seen any children. After a rather bizarre conversation, he told me about the clowns and meeting you and Damon and the others. Then he took off like a dog that has picked up a scent. I caught up with him and he told me we needed to wait here and that sooner or later you would appear."

As the hoards of children continued to clamber through the hole and gather in the field, Toshi filled Damon and Wynne in on recent events.

After the Witch Mother had watched Ariadne the Awful crumble to dust, she had explored the school. In a small room, coated in dust, amongst other papers dating back decades, she had discovered a hand-written note signed Sebastian Barthwhistle. The note had pleaded with the then much-respected witches of the Pentagram School to look after the Talisman of Evil. A further exploration of the school had unearthed a withered old man who claimed he had been living in the cellar for years, coming out twice a day to clean and cook for the children. From him the Witch Mother had gleaned more about the Talisman, including how, when Ariadne had taken control of the school, he had seen her claim the Talisman – then in the form of an oddly shaped cross – from its hiding place in the dank depths of the school. He had known it was something of huge importance from the way Ariadne had handled it, as if it were incredibly fragile. He had also seen, years later, Ariadne disguise the talisman as a giant lollipop, which she had clung to throughout the dark years when her madness had grown to its final terrifying proportions.

The Witch Mother had soon realised that the Talisman was no longer at the school, which led her to conclude that the escaping children had it.

"But how do you know all this, Toshi?" asked Wynne, picking lumps of earth from her hair.

"I happened to be perched outside the Pink Witch's house. Heard her talking on her crystal communicator. My hearing is very acute. We're not just ordinary birds, you know."

"We had noticed," said Damon, grinning. He had decided Toshi wasn't so bad after all – for a bird.

"I also heard the Pink Witch tell the Witch Mother to wait for her at the school – that she was going to fly out and get her and plan how they were going to trace the Talisman's whereabouts. It wouldn't have taken them long to work out where a group of frightened children would be heading, which is why you need to get to Misty Well as quickly as possible. Even if you have the Talisman, the Pink Witch thinks it's at Misty Well and she'll go to any lengths to get it."

"We haven't got it," said Wynne dismally. "I had it

but it's gone missing. If I'd known how important it was I would have taken better care of it."

"We'll worry about where it is later," said Toshi. "For now you need to get to Misty Well and warn Belinda the Beautiful. I should probably have gone straight there, but I was concerned about you once this gentleman told me about the clowns and how you had tried to follow them to the Circus of Lost Souls. I hope it wasn't an error of judgement that has cost lives."

"But it's still hours away, and you can't carry both of us," said Wynne.

"What about the carpet?" asked Damon.

"What carpet?" asked Wynne.

"The huge flying one that Magento made his last entrance on! The one Joe and Cameron have been carrying for the last hour!"

"Oh," said Wynne. "Do you know how to use it then? It seemed pretty lifeless once Magento disappeared."

Tutting to himself as always, Toshi waddled over to

the carpet, which lay in a roll on the grass just beyond the entrance to the underground world. Joe and Cameron were lying next to it, both shiny with sweat and breathing heavily.

"Looks like a pretty run-of-the-mill flying carpet to me," said Toshi. "If the rumours about Magento the Magnificent are true, he didn't have the power to create much magic of his own. The magic is inside the carpet itself. With ancient magic artefacts like this its usually just a matter of issuing commands."

"How do you mean exactly?" asked Damon, crouching next to Toshi.

"I command you to unfold," squawked Toshi. And the carpet stirred, wriggled like the chrysalis of a giant butterfly, then promptly flung itself flat across the grass, smothering Joe and Cameron who let out yells of surprise.

"Like that," said Toshi.

"So if we were to say 'carpet I command you take us to the village of Misty Well,' would it know where to go?" asked Wynne, stepping up alongside Damon.

"I presume so," replied Toshi, tutting thoughtfully. "It all depends on how powerful its creator was. Some magic carpets need to be told every little detail, while others do everything for you. Let's just hope this is one of the latter."

"Now we need to decide who's coming on the carpet," said Wynne, placing her hands on each hip as she always did when saying something of significance.

"Well I am for a start," said Damon, with some of his old pomposity.

"Of course," said Wynne. "But there's room for quite a few others on there."

"I'd like to come, if possible," said Joe, scrambling from under the carpet.

"And me!" came Cameron's muffled voice – he was still underneath the carpet.

"I think Molly should come with us too," said Damon, trying to sound as if Molly's safety was of only slight importance to him.

"I agree," said Wynne. "And the rest can make their

way to Misty Well on foot. Perhaps you could guide them?" she turned to the strange moss-covered man from the forest, who nodded. Despite his strangeness, there was something familiar about him that made Wynne believe he could be trusted.

"We'd better get moving," said Damon. "The Pink Witch and your awful mother may already be there."

The elected carpet riders stepped on board. Damon was about to give the necessary command when an ice-cold voice rose from amidst the gaggle of children.

"Not ssso fasssst!"

Kiskis slithered towards the carpet, his face a picture of rage.

"How dare you forget about me after all I've done for you. I go where you go, remember. I didn't help you because I care about you or any of your human friends, I did it because we had a deal – a deal you seem very happy to break now that you are back on the surface."

"Kiskis, I'm sorry, I didn't think," spluttered Damon,

recalling his initial terror on meeting the Mosstrol boy.

"Didn't think?" hissed Kiskis sliding onto the carpet, jagged teeth still bared. "Chose to forget more like. Hoped to get away without paying me back for all my favours."

"It wasn't like that," insisted Damon. Part of him wanted to give Kiskis a good shove, but his sensible side told him this might be a bad move.

"Just get this thing in the air!" ordered Kiskis. "Your apologies are wasted on me. I know when I've been cheated."

Damon realised there was no point arguing with Kiskis, so still shaky from the confrontation, he made the command and the carpet began to slowly rise. It was then that Damon remembered how terrified he was of heights. He sat in the middle of the carpet with his legs folded and closed his eyes. Wynne sat next to him and placed an arm around his shoulders, which he promptly shook off. "I'm fine," he lied. But as the carpet suddenly shot upwards and then forwards at a terrific speed he let out a startled shriek which left no doubt as to his fear.

2

The carpet had turned stiff and flat, like a sheet of plywood, which made sitting firmly upon it fairly easy. Still Damon kept his eyes squeezed shut, feeling leaves brush the bottom of the carpet as it soared just above the thick forest.

"Damon, it might be better to look," advised Wynne gently, resting a hand on his shoulder again.

"Shut up!" said Damon. "I'm just resting my eyes."

"You might make yourself feel sick," Wynne warned.

"I couldn't feel any sicker," fumed Damon, barely opening his mouth, so that his voice sounded robotic.

"Let him be sick," said Kiskis, still sulking at his near exclusion from the flying party.

Damon felt a small, warm body flop across his lap. He opened his eyes a crack and saw Molly draped there, thumb inserted neatly into her mouth, flushed cheeks puffing and deflating as she sucked contentedly.

"Wow!" cheered Cameron, who was lying flat on his front, so that his head protruded beyond the edge of the carpet – like a ship's figurehead.

"What?" asked Joe, who lay next to him, but further away from the edge, peering through one eye.

"It's the Royal Palace," Cameron pointed excitedly ahead and slightly to his right. "It must be – it's huge! And look at all the buildings around it. There are hundreds."

"It's called a city," said Kiskis.

"It's called a city," repeated Cameron in an exaggeratedly pompous tone. Kiskis scowled and returned to silent sulking.

"Can't we stop and have a look round?" asked Cameron. "I've always wanted to meet King Arold. He's supposed to be very funny."

"He's a joke all right,' said Wynne. "A drunken old joke who couldn't run from one end of the throne room to the other, let alone run a land with all the problems of

Lightsleep."

"You shouldn't talk about royalty like that," said Cameron.

"Well it's true," returned Wynne. "If he was any sort of king evil bags like the Pink Witch would never have managed to get so powerful and so feared. He's supposed to be a warlock, but he's always too drunk to speak any kind of incantation. If the Pink Witch does get hold of the Talisman of Evil she'll have no problem overthrowing him. Who'd stop her? His army are all as drunk as he is. They've got nothing else to do. He never holds any tournaments or inspects them or asks them for anything. He just wakes up, belches, drinks and falls asleep again."

"You know a lot about him seeing as you've never met him," said Kiskis.

"And you have I suppose," said Wynne, glancing at him moodily.

"Yes," said Kiskis, "While I was living under the palace. I was stealing wine from the cellar and he was splayed out on the floor…drunk."

"There you go then," said Wynne.

Soon the carpet had left the Royal Palace and the capital city of Lightsleep far behind and for a while the children were quiet, until Cameron let out another gasp – but this one contained no pleasure, only shock and fear.

"It's her!" he breathed, pointing again. "It's her!"

"Who?" Wynne squinted against the wind, trying to see what had disturbed Cameron. And then she did and she, too, gasped, gripping Damon's arm tightly so that he squealed and opened his eyes – opened them just in time to see two large grey shapes hovering some fifty feet to their right. The grey shapes, he soon realised, were stone gargoyles. Perched upon the back of one was the Witch Mother and a smaller figure draped in a black cloak. Sitting astride the other, and staring straight at them was the Pink Witch.

CHAPTER THIRTY

1

Damon realised that this was the first time he had seen the Pink Witch's face and the sight gave him his biggest shock since arriving in the magical land of Lightsleep.

"But she's beautiful!" he exclaimed, looking at Wynne accusingly. "You said she was ugly."

Wynne responded with a scowl, watching the gargoyles fly closer, their great wings creaking like rusty gate hinges. As they approached, the Pink Witch stood, her mane of candyfloss-coloured hair billowing around her. She had a face like one of the women from the TV show Damon had been watching on the morning he'd jumped through the floor in the room of pipes – a perfect face, with dainty features – not at all the hideous visage Wynne had suggested.

Soon the gargoyles and their passengers were no more then twenty feet away, flying alongside the carpet, the Pink Witch's gaze still focussed directly on the carpet riders.

"I'm scared," whispered Molly, peering through sleepy eyes at the hovering witches.

"Why doesn't she blast us?" asked Damon.

Wynne shrugged. "She probably doesn't know who we are. Mother won't have told her about us. She always swore to the Pink Witch that she didn't have any children. As far as she's concerned we're just a group of kids out for a leisurely ride."

Damon surveyed the group aboard the carpet, including Kiskis, who was vomiting forth some of his sticky webbing in case it was required in a fight with the witches.

"We hardly look like your average daytrippers," he said.

"I wonder who the other person is," said Wynne, nodding towards the small figure covered in the black cape.

"How should I know?" returned Damon. "I'm more interested in how we get away before the Pink Witch decides to blast us out of the sky."

But the Pink Witch remained some twenty feet away,

staring across at them, considering her next move.

"Maybe she doesn't want to blast us in case she damages the carpet," suggested Joe. "They're not exactly common and probably a lot easier to control than gargoyles."

"I think the gargoyles are more a fashion statement than a practical means of transportation," said Wynne, glancing nervously at the Pink Witch, whose perfect face was disfigured by a menacing scowl.

"We could try asking the carpet to go faster," said Cameron. "I bet it could out-run those great stone monstrosities any day."

Damon's stomach turned at the thought of more speed at this height.

"We'd better decide quickly," said Wynne, as the Pink Witch pointed a long white finger at the children.

"Carpet, fly ten times faster!" yelled Cameron. And there followed a gut-lurchingly awful few moments. As the carpet shot forwards, flinging all the children onto their backs, the Pink Witch sent forth a massive blast of magic energy. It crackled in the air like lightning, missing the children by inches. Everything round them, the sky, the forest, the fields all congealed into a paint-like mess as the carpet rocketed towards Misty Well.

Damon screamed and was so terrified, he didn't even think about what an embarrassing thing this was for a boy of his age to do. He closed his eyes to the streaming colours and gripped onto Molly. Whatever magic the carpet contained kept them on board, but the wind lashed across them and, just to make matters worse, it started to rain, and the drops hit their faces like thousands of needles.

And then everything calmed down. Damon heard Wynne give a happy squeal and felt the carpet come to a gentle stop and begin to sink towards the ground. He opened one eye, then the other and released a sigh of relief. The carpet was hovering just a few feet from the ground. They were in the midst of a small village, comprising several quaint cottages with thatched roofs around a village green, in the middle of which stood a large well. Above the well hung a thick cloud of mist.

"Is this Misty Well?" asked Damon. Wynne looked at him and shook her head in disbelief.

"At least I didn't ask 'What carpet?' when I suggested flying here on it!" called Damon as Wynne walked off towards the nearest cottage with the others in tow.

Damon scrambled to his feet, and ran after them. "You wait until the next time you say something stupid!"

Then he noticed a burning smell and turned to see the carpet smouldering and flapping like the wing of an injured bird. "Look!" he cried to the others. As they ran back the carpet burst into flames and began to curl and shrink like a crisp packet under a hot grill.

"The Pink Witch must have hit it," said Wynne sadly.

They stood and watched their magic mode of transport disintegrate, before silently following the cobbled lanes of Misty Well in search of Belinda the Beautiful.

Before they reached the cottages a ball of mist appeared above the cobbled road and out of it stepped a chubby, rosy-cheeked woman with dark brown hair cut into a neat bob. She was wearing a very ordinary pair of brown slacks, a beige jumper and what looked to Damon like a pair of well-worn trainers.

She waved casually to the children. "Hi, good to see you, I'm Belinda."

"You're a witch?" exclaimed Damon.

"That's not a term I like to use," said Belinda, frowning. "I prefer to say 'person of magical ability'. But let's not chat here. A lot has happened that you need to be filled in on. I presume you are Wynne and that you are Damon," she said looking from Wynne to Cameron."

"No, I'm Damon," said Damon, stepping forward.

"Oh," said Belinda, appearing confused.

"Why did you think he was me?" demanded Damon nodding towards Cameron.

"Sorry," said Belinda. "It's just that George said Damon was extremely brave. You just don't look like the type to fight bears and rescue people from wolves. I apologise for judging by appearances – most unlike me."

Damon opened his mouth to protest, but Belinda had already turned her back to him and was leading the way down the narrow lane between the idyllic cottages.

"Where are all the children?" asked Wynne. "I thought there were hundreds of children here."

"You'll see!" called Belinda. "And I prefer the term people of limited years – just a little rule of thumb we like to adhere to here."

"Bet there won't be any people of limited age like me here," said Kiskis.

Belinda stopped outside a small thatched cottage with bay windows split into neat squares.

"It's like a fairytale cottage," sighed Wynne, and Damon scowled at how girly she sounded. It was also rather bizarre hearing something in this impossible world considered special for being like something out of a fairytale. They'd met Red Riding Hood, after all!

Belinda smiled briefly and knocked on the dark wooden door with a large brass knocker shaped like a two-dimensional wishing well.

"Don't tell me you've packed all the kids in there!" exclaimed Damon.

Belinda looked down at him as if he were a little stupid.

The door opened and a boy none of them recognised peered out. He had a pale, chubby face with flushed cheeks and a sprinkling of freckles across his nose. One of his large brown eyes turned inwards, making it difficult to tell who he was looking at. He beamed when he saw Belinda and the others.

"They're here!" he called over his shoulder.

"We've been hearing all about you," the boy gabbled. "About the school and the Pink Witch and the Talisman of Evil. Can you believe Red Riding Hood has stolen it and gone to her…"

"That's enough, Russell," snapped Belinda. "I'm going to explain everything over a cup of herbal tea."

"Did he say Samantha had stolen the Talisman?" asked Wynne as Belinda led the way into the tiny cottage.

Damon nodded. "Can't say I'm surprised," he said. "I never did trust her."

"You didn't say anything," replied Wynne.

"I knew you'd just tell me I was too suspicious."

"I thought she was okay," said Joe.

"So did I," agreed Cameron, glancing around the room they found themselves in. It was massive; a huge dormitory with hundreds of beds lining the long white walls to their left and right.

"How…?" gasped Damon and he saw the others were equally as stunned.

"I can't take the credit," said Belinda, marching briskly ahead. "There was magic here at Misty Well long before I came here. It used to be the home to a number of powerful witches – people of magical ability. They left their magic in every stone and every blade of grass. Creating a massive space like this inside a small cottage was fairly simple with so much magic to draw on. The rate people of limited years are coming here I may have to create an extension soon."

Wynne coughed. "There's actually quite a few more coming," she said. "We freed them from an evil circus."

Belinda sighed. "I definitely need some herbal tea."

She led them through the deserted dormitory into a vast playroom, where contended children played with all manner of toys. There was none of the desperation that had filled the playroom at the Pentagram School.

"Wynne!" George was beaming from amongst a group of children constructing a tower from large coloured bricks. He ran over still waving. "You made it!" he cried giving Wynne a long hard hug. Wynne blushed and patted his back.

"So did you," she replied. "Well done for getting

everyone here."

"It was no problem," said George. "Molly, would you like to come and play?"

Molly nodded, although her drooping eyes suggested all she really wanted to do was sleep. She allowed George to lead her to the brick tower, waving lazily as she went.

The others followed Belinda into a small office off to the left of the playroom. It had a glass door, bearing a plaque that read 'Belinda the Beautiful's Office'.

"One of the students made it," said Belinda without even looking back at the children's smiling faces. "I didn't want to offend her."

Inside the office was a simple desk and several hard wooden chairs.

"Take a seat everyone," said Belinda, gesturing towards the chairs and sitting herself down at the desk.

The children began to chat animatedly about their recent adventure on the carpet and the revelations about Samantha.

"We've a lot to discuss so it would help if we left idle chatter for another time," said Belinda firmly. The children all stopped talking at once and fixed polite gazes on the witch – person of magical ability. Even Kiskis, who was pouting as best he could with his thin grey lips, did not answer back.

"Tea first," announced Belinda, snapping her fingers. Steaming mugs appeared in front each of the children and one particularly large mug materialised in front of her.

Damon wrinkled his nose at the smell rising from his mug, while Kiskis began to lap at his brew enthusiastically. The remaining children gave their drinks polite sips.

"It's actually not bad," said Cameron. "Nice in fact," and he began to drink with more gusto.

"You'll feel much better for drinking it," advised Belinda, eyeing Damon who was still to try his. "Now the first matter to discuss is Samantha – or Red Riding Hood", she continued. "I'm afraid fear got the better of her earlier today. The Pink Witch paid us a visit. She didn't get too close of course. She'd never get that near to a village populated by people of limited...I'll just say children for the sake of speed, but I don't generally like the term – rather patronising, I always feel. Anyway, the Pink Witch stayed on her gargoyle and shouted down to us. She demanded that we surrender the Talisman of Evil or suffer her displeasure. She said she would wait at the circle of stone about a mile away in the forest but that if no-one came within three hours with the Talisman she would return and destroy Misty Well.

"We didn't even realise at the time that we had the Talisman of Evil, but after the Pink Witch left Samantha began to act very strangely. George saw her creeping out an hour or so later. He noticed she was carrying Ariadne's lollipop. I put two and two together and realised the lollipop was the Talisman.

"A small group of us tried to give chase, but I daren't stray far from Misty Well and Samantha is very expert at losing herself in woods."

"Why did she do it?" asked Wynne. "She seemed so

nice."

"She was terrified," said Belinda, the steam from her tea rising in front of her face, giving her already red cheeks an even brighter glow. "She'd seen her friends disappear in front of her eyes. She realised she wasn't real, that she was just something temporary conjured up by a demented witch. I guess she hoped the Pink Witch would help her in return for the Talisman. I'm afraid Samantha will learn a harsh lesson – it would be unheard of for the Pink Witch to help anyone."

"Poor Samantha," sighed Wynne.

"Poor Samantha!" scoffed Damon. "How can you feel sorry for her?"

"She couldn't help being scared," said Joe. "There were times when I was terrified at Ariadne's school. I would have done just about anything to get away."

"But you didn't," said Cameron. "None of us would have ever turned traitor to get away."

"Exactly," said Damon. "I hope she flickers out before she even gets to the Pink Witch."

"Well I think you could all try and be a bit more understanding," said Wynne. "She was good to us before all this 'fictional character' stuff cropped up."

"I admire your compassion, Wynne," said Belinda, "But you may not feel quite so sympathetic towards Red Riding Hood if the Pink Witch uses the Talisman to take over Lightsleep and condemns every child to slavery – or worse."

Wynne looked down into her mug of tea.

"What has she got against kids anyway?" asked Damon.

"Kids are baby goats, " said Belinda.

"Whatever," said Damon.

"The answer to your question is a bleak tale," said Belinda, steam settling on her glasses, hiding her bright eyes. She was silent for a second or two.

"Are you going to tell us or not?" Damon demanded.

Belinda looked up and wiped the steam from her round lenses. "The Pink Witch wasn't always quite as horrible as she is now," she began. "At least it wasn't always quite so obvious how vile she was. She was the devoted daughter of Irwin Yucklewit, a warlock and wealthy lord. He owned the house where the Pink Witch still lives, although it wasn't pink then. The Pink Witch's mother died when she was just a young girl. It wasn't this that turned her. She was a nasty child before and after her mother's death. It was her father she doted on, and with his wife dead all he had in his life was his daughter, magic and money. Although he was a hard man he spoilt his daughter terribly. Everything that young Agnes – that's her real name – wanted she got. She developed an even more hateful, despicable personality than the one she already had. She treated her peers with utter disdain."

"What did she have against pears?" asked Damon.

Wynne burst into hysterical cackles.

"What?" asked Damon bemused.

"Peers, Damon," said Belinda, "Not pears. People of her own age."

"Oh," said Damon, blushing and scowling at Wynne.

Belinda went on: "These peers included her younger sister, who barely deserves a mention in this story because she hardly played any part in the events I'm describing. She was a dumpy, plain child of little note anyway, so it's no great loss to the tale."

Belinda coughed and then continued: "By the time Agnes had grown into a woman she had no friends at all. Her father continued to spoil her as if she were still his little girl until the day he died. It was his passing that caused something in Agnes to twist, to warp. And the self-centred, utterly nasty woman turned into a completely evil witch – and in this case the description is a fair one. She spent years studying the dark arts, while converting her father's stately home into a monstrous pink shrine to vanity.

"And then she met Peter Petabrill. He was a stunningly handsome student of wizardry who had come in search of her father. He had travelled from across The Water, and his dark skin and deep brown eyes seemed exotic and romantic to the Pink Witch. Despite her attraction to the stranger she had initially treated him with the same lack of respect she showed everyone but even she was not immune to his dark penetrating stare and deep musical voice and, to everyone's amazement, Peter and the Pink Witch were married within months of their first meeting. He was as blinded by her surface beauty as she was by his.

"All went well for a few years. People in the surrounding villages almost forgot she was there until the night she gave birth to the twins and her screams filled the night – mad, bitter, gut-churning screams.

"The twins became Peter's pride and joy. He became as devoted to them as he had initially been to his wife. The Pink Witch's hatred for the children grew as rapidly as his love. She managed to hide it in Peter's presence, but when he was forced to return home over The Water for a few months on family business, the Pink Witch lost all control. The jealousy and venom she had stifled for ten years exploded and she locked her own children inside the dark secret passages that ran inside the walls of the house and left them there to starve."

"That's awful!" gasped Wynne.

"I met them!" interjected Damon, his voice shaking. "I met their ghosts inside the Pink Witch's house. Their names were Arthur and Catherine."

Belinda nodded. "When Peter returned and discovered what she had done he locked himself alone in a room and cried for days, calling out the names of his beloved children. Then one morning he emerged from the room, his face red and swollen with grief, his eyes filled with hatred. He pointed a shaking finger at his wife. 'I curse you!' he spat. 'I curse you until the day you die for what you have done. You will never go near a child again. If a child so much as touches you, it will feel as if a red hot poker is being plunged into your flesh.' The Pink Witch felt the power of the curse swell inside her until she couldn't breath and she fell to the floor in a faint. When she came round Peter had gone, never to return – at least this is how the story is told. No-one was actually there to see any of this."

"It's a shame he didn't just kill her," said Damon. And this time nobody argued.

"And that's all the time we have for stories," said Belinda, draining her mug and standing. "Now we have to decide which of you brave people is going to go to the Pink Witch's house to steal back the Talisman of Evil before she uses it to take over Lightsleep."

CHAPTER THIRTY-ONE

1

There followed a fear-filled silence, finally broken by Cameron, who asked: "Can't we all go?"

Belinda shook her head gravely. "I can create a portal of magical mist to send two of you, but anything more powerful than that would take at least a couple of hours to conjure up, and we just don't have that sort of time."

"Can't you just keep conjuring up less powerful ones and send us through two at a time?" asked Joe.

"Unfortunately it doesn't work like that," said Belinda. "The magic of Misty Well operates to long-forgotten mystic rules. I can use the magical mist to move around Misty Well as often as I like, but for whatever reason, I can only conjure it twice in a day to take people in or out of the village – in this case once to send the chosen two out and once to get them back again. So I'm afraid you must decide amongst yourselves which two will go."

"Can't you go?" asked Damon. "You're the witch."

Belinda removed her spectacles and polished the lenses one after the other on an over-long sleeve even though they blatantly didn't need cleaning. "Person of magical ability," she said. "And I'm needed here."

"Oh and babysitting a few kids is more important than saving Lightsleep is it?" demanded Damon. "Does someone desperately need a bath, or is some boy's nose running? How can you send two of us off to fight the Pink Witch after everything you've told us about her?"

"I don't have power like Agnes," said Belinda, although she was staring at the top of her desk rather than at Damon. "My power comes from this place. Outside of the village I'm just a beginner. I've never amounted to anything more than a beginner. I could entertain you with a few tricks, but she has magic running through her veins. She can blast it from her fingertips or breathe it like fire. I can't compete with that."

"But we can?" asked Damon.

"I've been here for nearly ninety years," said Belinda. "I don't even know if I can live beyond Misty Well. My work has always kept me here."

"And you've done a great job," said Wynne before Damon could respond with any more accusations.

"Thank you," said Belinda. "But I do it for the young people, not for gratitude. It kills me to send two of you off to fight that woman, but what is the alternative?"

"I'll go," said Wynne.

And me," said Cameron, standing as if to leave immediately.

"She's my sister," exclaimed Damon. "If anyone's going with her, it's me!"

Wynne stared at him open mouthed.

"What?" Damon snapped at her.

"Nothing," replied Wynne quietly.

"I think that's the right choice," said Belinda with a mixture of resolution and sadness.

2

Within minutes a large mass of children had congregated by the well in the middle of the village green. Standing closest to the well, their faces blurred by the dusk, were the children that had traveled with Wynne and Damon from the Pentagram School. George, looking concerned, Molly, her small hands reaching out to stroke Damon's arm; Joe and Cameron standing resiliently together as if to take on the challenge should Damon and Wynne have a sudden change of heart and many other faces, all etched with a mixture of worry and pride.

They chatted nervously until Belinda raised her hands and silence fell.

"I need you all to be very quiet while I conjure the portal," she said, her voice loud and seemingly calm. "The lives of these children depend on how strong I can make it." She turned to Damon and Wynne. "You will need to move the instant the portal is formed. I will only be able to sustain it for a few seconds over such a distance. If I have calculated

309

right you should step out in the woods just a short walk from the Pink Witch's house."

Damon and Wynne nodded, their faces sombre.

"If at any time you feel you can't cope or if you have the Talisman of Evil and need to get back, just call me on this." She handed Damon what looked like a test tube but with no opening.

"It's a portable crystal," said Wynne reading Damon's expression. "One of the more modern models."

Damon shrugged and handed it to Wynne, hoping she knew how to use it.

"Good luck both of you," said George.

"Yeah, good luck," said Cameron patting Damon's back.

Joe stepped up to Wynne. "Take care," he said softly. He was blushing and looking from Wynne's face to the ground. "I'll be thinking of you every second you're away."

Wynne blushed too. "Thank you," she said and impulsively she leant forward and kissed his smooth, cold cheek, making him blush even redder. Wynne felt her legs grow a little wobbly.

Belinda had begun to mumble an incantation, her arms stretched across the opening of the well.

"What about me?" came a rattling voice from the back of the crowd, and Belinda paused, looking vexed.

Kiskis slithered through the parting children. "When do I get to go home?" he demanded. "That's why I'm here, because I thought this well could get me back to my world."

"Now is not the time to talk about that!" snapped Belinda. "Slither back to where you came from and let me send these children off to save all our futures."

Kiskis hissed and slithered back a few feet.

Belinda turned back to the well. "Don't forget," she said. "You must jump straight through the second the portal appears."

And she began to chant again, hands suspended above the well, almost invisible within the cloud of mist. Soon the cloud began to swirl and a snake-like wisp rose and curled its way across and down so that the end rested on the grass next to the well. Belinda continued to chant, her eyes open wide. The strand of mist began to expand and in its midst a darkness formed, a whirling, tunnel of darkness like a miniature black hole.

"Now!" shouted Belinda and Wynne and Damon leapt into the darkness, their hands tightly clasped.

3

They each felt a sensation of falling which made their hearts stop for a second, then they were stepping out into the forest and ahead of them, between the trees, they saw a flash of bright pink.

"Her house," said Wynne, clutching her stomach, which felt queasy.

"I know it's her house," said Damon grumpily, but Wynne didn't react. She realised Damon was frightened and that being moody was his way of trying to hide it.

"How are we going to get in?" she asked. "I'll bet she'll have sealed up all the windows with magic since your last visit."

"I've already thought about that," said Damon, sounding slightly smug. "When I escaped before I climbed up a chimney. I think that's the best way in."

"And how do we get onto the roof?" asked Wynne, as they crept closer to the house, aware of every cracking twig or rustle of leaves beneath their feet. Somehow everything seemed louder in the dark.

"That's the bit I haven't thought of," confessed Damon.

"We could do with Toshi or Heeshee," said Wynne, looking wistfully upwards.

"Or Kiskis," said Damon. "He could puke up some of that web stuff and make a rope."

"Or the magic carpet," said Wynne.

As they reached the edge of the forest an owl hooted loudly above their heads and Damon shivered.

"Are you okay?" asked Wynne.

"I'm fine, just thinking about how to get onto the roof."

Wynne looked up at the garish slates that formed the roof of the Pink Witch's house. "I suppose there's no way you could..."

"Fly?"

Wynne nodded.

"I could try," said Damon. "I managed it at the circus."

"It would be a great help if you could," said Wynne.

"I realise that," said Damon." Stop talking for a minute while I concentrate."

Wynne fell silent. Damon focused all his attention on the idea of flying, trying to recreate the feeling of rising from the ground at the Circus of Lost Souls. It had happened easily then but now there was not even a glimmer of the flying sensation. He closed his eyes and felt Wynne slip her hand back into his. He pictured the roof way above their heads and how much he needed to be up there. "Come on," he willed himself. "You've done it before."

Wynne let out a small gasp, but he continued to concentrate on the idea of being on the roof, of floating up there slowly and gently.

"Damon?"

"What?" He opened his eyes and turned to face Wynne, ready to insist she keep quiet and realised they were twenty feet above the ground. He felt the familiar lurching sensation in his stomach but forced himself to stay calm and move slowly forward towards the roof.

His style was far more graceful than during his original flight – more like floating than flying with none of the frantic leg and arm flapping.

They drew level with the lowest of the house's many roofs and stepped onto the lurid tiles.

"Well done!" cried Wynne, squeezing Damon's hand.

Damon snatched it free. "It was easy," he said. "Now let's find a chimney big enough for us to fit down."

As they climbed the slope of the roof they heard a familiar sound – a sound like rusty gate hinges. For a second or two they couldn't remember where they had heard it before and why it made the hairs on the back of their necks prickle. Then they glanced at each other, both crouched like cats, and each saw realisation dawn in the other's eyes.

"Gargoyles," they whispered together and snapped their gazes upwards.

The dark sky appeared gargoyle-free. Damon looked to his right trying to detect the source of the grating noise and saw, about fifty yards away, two large grey shapes, their passengers outlined against the blue/white moon.

The Pink Witch was standing astride hers like a malevolent circus performer. Damon imagined her circling the ring of the Circus of the Lost Souls, soulless children clapping, their blank eyes staring straight ahead.

"She'll see us as soon as they turn this way!" hissed Wynne.

But the Pink Witch and her mount did not head towards the house. They kept flying, the heavy wings of both gargoyles lifting and falling with painful slowness.

"Where is she going?" asked Wynne.

They kept low on the roof, relying on the darkness to hide them as they watched the Pink Witch and her small entourage fly on.

"My house!" blurted Wynne. "Why would she come here when the pure evil is kept at my house?"

"And you've only just thought of that!" asked Damon.

"At least I thought of it!"

"Too late! How do we get to your house now?"

"Well maybe we could fly if you'd just get a grip and do it without making such a drama out of it!" stormed Wynne.

"You fly us there if it's that easy!".

"Don't shout at me!" Wynne gave Damon a small shove. Gentle though it was, the shove caught Damon off-balance and to Wynne's utter horror he fell backwards and over the edge of the roof.

"Damon!" Wynne scrambled down the roof, tears already streaming down her face.

"What?" asked Damon moodily, his head appearing above the gutter.

"Are you okay?" asked Wynne, quickly wiping away the tears.

"No thanks to you. Shall we go?"

Without waiting for a reply Damon caught hold of Wynne's arm and lifted her into the night sky.

4

Flying had finally become the soaring, exhilarating experience Damon had imagined it would be. He felt weightless, as did Wynne, as if his power was seeping through his hand into hers. They rode the gentle air currents,

318

arms spread, legs trailing behind them. There was no fear of heights now. He felt that even if he did fall, he would do so slowly and gracefully like a feather.

The euphoric feeling died suddenly as Wynne's house came into view. Seeing the great mass of gothic spires and towers and smoking chimneys, Damon wondered how he could ever have thought it resembled his own modest home. He felt a pain in his chest at the memory of the small semi-detached house and of his mother. He wondered, just for a moment, if he would ever see her again.

Perched on top of one of the towers were the two gargoyles, their wings folded on their cold, broad backs, their grotesque faces cast downwards.

"They're already inside," said Wynne. "We have to stop them."

But her attention was suddenly caught by a figure, a red caped figure running along the track towards the house.

"Samantha!" said Wynne, pointing.

"Let's get her!" shouted Damon, swooping down towards the traitor.

Samantha screamed as Damon and Wynne alighted before her. In her shock she tripped and fell, red hood falling across her face. "Don't hate me!" she begged. "I'm sorry."

Damon glared at the cowering form, but made no move to either attack or comfort her.

Wynne took a step towards her and reached out a hand as if to rest it on the other girl's head. But before she could offer this small token of forgiveness Samantha, Red Riding Hood, disappeared.

"Samantha?" Wynne called, staring at the empty space, and suddenly she was there again, but fainter, her outline flickering. Wynne could see through her crouching form to the path beyond. Samantha looked up, her transparent face streaked with dirty tears. "I just wanted to be real," she sobbed. "She said she would help me, but as soon as the house came into view she laughed and told the other witch to push me off the gargoyle. I hit the ground so hard, but guess what?"

"What?" asked Wynne.

"It didn't hurt. I just stood up and brushed the mud off of my cape as if I'd tripped down a step. That's when I knew for sure I was just something made up – something created in the head of a mad witch because she was bored one day."

Samantha broke into louder sobs, her outline flickering more wildly like an image from a badly tuned TV.

"You weren't just a thing to us," said Wynne. "You were our friend. You gathered food for us and helped lead the children to Misty Well. You just went a bit wrong towards the end."

Samantha sniffed and wiped her eyes on the hem of her cape. "It is the end isn't it," she said, her voice growing faint.

"I think so," admitted Wynne and she stroked Samantha's pale face. Except there was no face to stroke, just an empty space and the warm trickle of a tear running down the back of Wynne's hand.

Wynne felt tears of her own well in her eyes, but Damon pulled her along the path towards the house. "Come on," he coaxed. "There's no time for crying over her. She wasn't even a real person."

"You're so hard-faced sometimes," said Wynne.

"One of us has to be."

"Oh, like you were when we got stuck up that tree and had to sit there for hours because you were too scared to get us down – oh you were really hard then. Such a big tough guy."

"Shut up," snapped Damon. "Why do you always have to answer back? Don't you think we should be worrying about how to stop the Pink Witch and your mad mother rather than arguing?"

His final words were drowned by a huge, night-shattering roar. Both children looked towards the house. Rising from the roof, perhaps a hundred feet high, was a monstrous, dark form. It was shaped like the top half of a man, but a hideously deformed man – a great gaping mouth, drooling long strings of black gunge, hair like a crown of writhing serpents, powerful arms and hands that groped at the air as if to rip through it with vicious talons. It roared again, head thrown back, eyes blazing red.

"I think we left it too late," said Damon.

CHAPTER THIRTY-TWO

1

The hallway seemed chillier and more cavernous than ever. The walls, mounted with flickering torches, were alive with dancing shadows. Beyond the wide stairway more doors had appeared, some open, revealing dark musty rooms, others closed and rattling in their frames as the commotion on the roof shook the house.

"What now?" asked Damon, pausing at the foot of the stairs, attempting to digest the new developments. He tried to remember his first day in Lightsleep and how for the first few seconds he had been unaware that he was even in another world. It seemed impossible now. Damon guessed that magic had played a part in easing his transition to this bizarre land.

"Come on," said Wynne, leading the way up the first flight of stairs. Damon followed her through the maze of corridors and up endless stairways, some so wide an elephant could easily have climbed them, some so narrow the children had to walk single file, their shoulders brushing the walls on each side. All the time the monster of pure evil raged above them.

Finally, they stood at the bottom of a winding stairway that curled around the inside of a tower. Wynne took the stairs two at a time and Damon followed.

At the top of the tower was a small landing and ahead of them a sturdy, dark wooden door with a dull metal handle shaped like a bat. Beyond the door the noise was deafening – a combination of the monster's wet, rattling roars and the hysterical shrieks of the Pink Witch as she celebrated her success.

"How are we going to stop that thing?" asked Damon.

"I have no idea," said Wynne, taking hold of the door handle.

2

In the forest less than half a mile away, Heeshee draped her soft white wing over her newly hatched children – six of them, all squawking their demands for more food. Toshi sat on the branch a short way from the nest, gazing across the fields to Wynne's house and the creature rising from it.

"I have to do something," he said.

"What can you do?" asked his wife. "It's gone too far for you to help. Your place is here with your children. We did everything we could."

Toshi knew his wife didn't mean what she said. She wasn't the type to sit back and let events take their course – not evil events. But like him she felt powerless.

I have to try," he said. "I can't leave them to fight that thing alone."

"You do what you feel you have to do," said Heeshee. "I don't have a choice. Just make sure you come back. I'm not raising this lot on my own."

"I will," said Toshi. "I love you."

And without giving himself time to change his mind, he took off and flew towards the scene of mayhem.

3

The noise as they opened the door was overpowering. The cries of the evil creature sounded like those of a legion of deranged demons. It was a dark, diseased sound.

"I can't stand this," shouted Damon, as they stepped out onto the parapet of the tower.

Wynne was blocking her ears, glancing around for a sign of the Pink Witch or her mother. They were shielded from the monster by the walls of the inside of the tower, but it rose above them, facing out across the forest, ready to burn it to the ground with a blast from its blazing red eyes.

They found the Witch Mother first, sitting with her back to the outside wall of the tower. She appeared stunned and drowsy.

"Mother?" Wynne hurried to the witch's side.

"Wynne?" The woman reached out a bony hand to her daughter, who clasped it in her own. "Wynne, what's happening?"

"Don't you know?" asked Wynne.

"You look so grown up," said her mother, squinting at her through weary eyes. "I know you're supposed to be this age, but I can't remember you growing up. I feel like I've dreamed the past few years."

"When did you start to feel like this?" asked Wynne, feeling her mother's hot forehead.

"When the Pink Witch lifted up the Talisman and called for the pure evil to take shape and do her bidding. I felt something force its way out of me It rose up from my stomach and out through my mouth. It was like a ball of black treacle. It flew to the pure evil and joined with it."

"I knew it," said Wynne. "The Pink Witch must have tricked you into eating some of the pure evil. That's why you turned so horrible. I kept telling people you hadn't always been that bad – you were never exactly a traditional mother, but you always seemed to care."

"She can help us now," said Damon, crouching at Wynne's side.

The Witch Mother frowned at him. "You're not my son are you?" she asked.

"No," said Damon. "I'm from another world. I seem to have borrowed your son's body for a while – at least I hope it's only a while."

"I've heard of that," said the Witch Mother. "Some people have counterparts in the other worlds and can transfer their spirits between bodies. Did one of the In-betweeners bring you?"

"We need to stop the Pink Witch and that thing," said Wynne, before her mother's thoughts could wander further.

"I don't know how," said the Witch Mother. "Unless you can get hold of the Talisman of Evil. If you have that you should be able to control the monster, but she isn't going to give it up easily. She plans to travel through Lightsleep letting the monster feed on all the evil, growing more and more powerful, and then claim the throne from King Arold."

They saw the Pink Witch now, balanced on the turret of the castle, arms raised high, the Talisman was now a shaft of dark metal with a circle fixed in its centre, blazing like a small sun. She was swamped by the massive black thing, of which she was now mistress, as it wailed and roared, thrashing its head from side to side like a caged animal that longed to be freed.

And then the Pink Witch turned and stared straight at Damon and a terrifying leer spread across her face.

"The boy from the other world," she said. "I felt you arrive. I knew you'd been in my house and stolen my book. You leave a trail like a snail. Are you supposed to stop me? Is that why the In-betweeners sent you? Are you one of the chosen ones? One of the special people?"

Damon shook his head, but couldn't speak.

"You don't look too special to me. You look like a frightened little boy."

Damon stood, his legs weak and shaking. "I'm not frightened of you," he said, but his quivering voice betrayed him.

"Damon, be careful," said Wynne.

"We came here to stop her, didn't we?" said Damon.

"I wish I knew when you were planning to be a hero," said Wynne, also standing. "If you could just be a bit more consistent I'd know what to expect."

"Shut up," said Damon. "We've got a maniac witch to fight."

"And a creature of pure evil," Wynne reminded him.

"Touch her," came the frail voice of the Witch Mother. "Touch her face. She can't stand to be touched by children."

"Easier said than done," replied Damon, staring at the poised figure of the Pink Witch, her wild pink hair fluttering around her beautiful, hard face.

And then her bright lips parted and she hissed two words in a voice as cold as winter wind. "Get them!"

"I think we should run," said Wynne, as the creature of pure evil turned and reached out a deadly hand to grab them.

The Witch Mother clambered to her feet. "Come on!" she called, pulling Wynne, who in turn pulled Damon back towards the door to the tower. Behind them the creature rose through the roof like thick, almost solid smoke. Legs like gnarled trees emerged through the grey tiles and the creature climbed over the castle turret, a massive hunting beast.

They reached the door, but their hearts sank. It was closed and there was no handle on their side. They were trapped and the creature of pure evil was bearing down on them, swamping them with its rancid breath.

And then Damon remembered his power and as the beast reached for them he grabbed Wynne and the Witch Mother and ran to the edge of the tower, leaping into the air as the monster's hand swiped.

The Witch Mother shrieked as they shot into the air, rising high above the house and even the monster, which was now sniffing around the parapet, was confused as to how it had lost its prey.

They hovered in mid-air, waiting for the monster to make its next move.

The Witch Mother clasped a white hand to her chest. "You really are one of the chosen ones," she said.

"What chosen ones?" asked Damon.

"I don't know all the details," replied the Witch Mother, between rasping breaths. "But it's all written down somewhere, in books older than this world. There are certain people who exist in all four worlds. Like I said before, they can swap bodies – that's obviously what you've done. But you must be from the Central World, the one of which Lightsleep – and the others – is just an echo. When someone from the Central World crosses over into one of the echo worlds they develop powers like flying, and many more. Their spirits become lighter, they are shocked into realising

333

their potential once out of the materialistic Central World, you see."

"I don't know what you're talking about," said Damon. "And it might be an idea to continue this conversation another time."

Below them the creature had realised how he had been duped. The Pink Witch was pointing up at them and the monster was rising into the air to carry out her bidding.

"It can fly too," said Damon.

"Fly down," said Wynne.

"Are you mad!" Damon glared at her. "I'll try and lose it in the forest."

"No Damon!" called Wynne, but he was already zooming towards the dense woodland, the Witch Mother and Wynne silenced by the jet of cold air that bit into their faces.

As they reached the edge of the forest, Damon dived amongst the trees, dodging between them with an expert precision that would have seemed impossible just hours earlier.

A cacophony of cracking and tearing announced the arrival of the monster and as the three of them glanced back they saw it sinking to the forest floor, crouching so that its head was just below the top of the tallest tree.

"Damon, we have to lead it away from here," said Wynne, as Damon paused, floating a few feet from the ground.

"Why?" he demanded.

"Imagine the destruction that thing will cause if it chases us through the forest. Thousands of animals could die – Heeshee and Toshi included."

Damon hadn't even considered this possibility.

"What do you suggest then?" he asked, as the monster began to crawl across the forest floor towards them, trees bending and creaking as it came.

"Fly back and straight towards the Pink Witch. It's the only way. We have to get the Talisman. We can't fight that thing, we have to control it."

"She's right," agreed the Witch Mother.

Damon glared at her. "Since when were you in charge around here?"

He noticed as he stared angrily into her face that since losing the piece of pure evil implanted by the Pink Witch, Wynne's mother more than ever resembled his own. He recognised the hazel eyes and the pale skin, the faint creases around the small mouth, and his anger evaporated.

He glanced at the prowling creature then with a defeated sigh, shot upwards and out of the forest. The creature followed, crashing through the canopy of the forest just ahead of them.

Damon took a deep breath and flew higher, then forwards at such a speed he was blinded for a few seconds.

When he stopped, opened his streaming eyes and glanced around, he saw the monster a short way behind and the Witch Mother's house below them once again.

"Here goes!" he announced and gripping the hands of his passengers, he dived downwards, air rushing through his ears, filling his lungs until he couldn't breathe. And then the Pink Witch was just a few feet away, her flint-like eyes fixed on his.

"Keep away!" she warned, "or I'll blast you!"

Damon dropped Wynne and the Witch Mother onto the tower roof. "Try and get inside," he said. "Break the door down if you have to."

"I'm not leaving you," said Wynne.

"If we split up the monster won't know who to chase. It's the best way."

Damon turned his attention back to the Pink Witch, who was watching the approach of her evil charge with an expression of glee.

"Come get the nasty little brat!" she called. Her fingers were twitching as if preparing to use her magic should her new charge fail her.

Damon leapt forward before the Pink Witch could react and grabbed her face between both his hands. She screamed as a sizzling sound emerged from under Damon's palms and the smell of meat cooking rose between his fingers. The Talisman of Evil clattered to the ground and as it clanged against the stone a shadow past over it. At first Damon thought it was the hand of the monster, but when he looked up he saw Toshi swoop down, grab the Talisman in his claw and take off again, just as a massive black claw made a grab for him.

Damon took his hands from the Pink Witch's face, the smell of burning was making him feel sick, as was the idea of inflicting such pain on somebody. The Pink Witch's skin was blackened and erupting with blisters that popped and crackled like the skin of a cooking chicken.

'You evil brat!" she screamed lashing out with her sharp pink nails. "I should have killed you straight away. Evil, nasty, stinking child!"

Pink light glowed around one of her outstretched hands, Damon backed away. The witch shuffled forwards, eyes blazing through her charred skin. "Wretched, selfish, brat," she hissed and blasted Damon with a bolt of pure magic. He screamed as it hit him square in the chest sending him crashing against the wall of the tower. He heard Wynne cry out, but it was a distant, dreamy sound. His head swam as the Pink Witch moved in for a second attack.

"Putrid, rancid, venomous monster," she chanted and released another magic blast which slammed Damon against the wall. Stone crumbled, showering him with dust, partially blinding him, but still he remained conscious.

"Why don't you die?" hissed the Pink Witch.

"Absorb her magic," a voice whispered inside his head. "Next time she hits you don't let it hurt, use it."

Damon didn't have time to decide whether or not he recognised the voice, as another blast of magic hit him, sending him crashing through the tower wall and plummeting towards the ground.

"Absorb it!" demanded the voice and Damon pictured the magic filling his body, from his feet to his head, warming him like a hot drink.

He felt suddenly strong, powerful. "I can destroy her," he thought, his head instantly clearing.

Damon stopped falling just feet from the ground and began to rise.

Soon he was level with the tower. He saw Toshi hovering way above him, still gripping the Talisman. He saw Wynne and the Witch Mother huddled by the door and the Monster frozen in mid air, waiting for the Talisman's new owner to command it.

He continued to rise, seeing the Pink Witch below glaring at him with a mixture of hatred and disbelief.

"Hi, Toshi," he greeted, drawing alongside the stunned bird and taking the Talisman. "I thought you might show up at some point."

Toshi tutted. "I could hardly leave you to deal with this on your own."

"I would have managed," said Damon, as a blast of magic energy crackled past his ear, missing him by less than an inch.

A strange ripping sound suddenly filled the air.

"What's that?" asked Damon.

Toshi tutted and flapped a wing towards the Pink Witch.

Something bizarre, and judging from the witch's screams, incredibly painful, was happening to her. She was growing, her neck stretching, burnt head bobbing on the end of it; her legs were creaking like old timber, veins and tendons bulging, as the limbs thickened and grew into great, muscular trunks; her arms too began to grow into gnarled branches, the skin stretching and tearing.

"Help me!" she screamed, her mouth filled with blood and great jagged teeth.

"What's happening to her?" asked Damon.

"I can only hazard a guess," said Toshi, "that when you touched her, you triggered off some kind of curse."

"Belinda said something about that," said Damon, watching horrified as the transformation of the Pink Witch continued. "She said the Pink Witch's husband cursed her and swore she'd never touch another child again."

341

"I'll hazard one other guess," said Toshi. "That the curse involved the Pink Witch's vanity and her ugly personality. I think what we're seeing here is her ugly inside taking shape."

"She sure is ugly," said Damon, as the monster that had been the beautiful Agnes let out a piercing shriek that sent birds flying from the forest and set wolves howling. She now stood at least twenty feet tall, hands clenched into enormous fists, which she pounded against the nearest turret in pain and frustration. The house creaked beneath her.

"What shall I do?" asked Damon.

"You said you could cope," replied Toshi.

Another blast of magic scored a central parting through Damon's hair. The Pink Witch was staring at him through big, dark eyes, full of loathing.

"How do I use this thing?" Damon held the Talisman in front of him.

"I suppose you just issue a command and it will make the pure evil do as you want it to do," said Toshi. "It's like the carpet, it has all the magic needed, you don't have to be magic to use it."

The pair leapt to one side in order to avoid the latest blast of magic.

"Now might be a good time to try it," suggested Toshi.

Damon shrugged. "I command the pure evil to attack the Pink Witch," he called.

"Is that such a good idea?" asked Toshi. "Imagine the devastation a fight between those two could cause."

But the monster was already reaching out for the Pink Witch, claws raking at her now bark-like skin, tearing at the remnants of her garish dress that hung in tatters from her inhuman body.

The Pink Witch swung a fist at the monster's jaw, knocking the creature backwards through what was left of the parapet. It roared and flailed in mid-air, finally righting itself and rising to face its foe.

Damon saw Wynne and the Witch Mother trying to break open the tower door with a large piece of stone they held between them.

The monster leapt for the Pink Witch's elongated throat, gripping it between its hands and squeezing, its massive jaw clenched with the effort.

The Pink Witch grabbed the monster by its throat and applied equal pressure. The two abominations staggered across the remains of the parapet, until it finally gave way, sending them plummeting towards the ground.

A crash and mighty tremor announced their landing.

Damon and Toshi looked at each other then flew over the house until they hovered above the felled pair of monsters.

For a moment the two huge bodies lay motionless, then the thing that had been the Pink Witch twitched and shuddered, pushing itself up onto all fours and then standing. It looked upwards, eyes once again resting on Damon.

"I'll get you!" it screamed in a voice that still resembled that of the Pink Witch, but was even more terrifying.

The monster of pure evil was also clambering to its feet, claws again ripping at the Pink Witch's flesh. She blasted it backwards with a bolt of magic, sending it crashing through the nearest wall.

The Pink Witch leapt into the air, letting out another painful screech. Damon and Toshi heard a familiar creaking sound and the Pink Witch's stone gargoyles rose up above the tower. The Pink Witch landed like the beast she now was, upon their backs, one gigantic foot resting on each.

"Fly!" she bellowed, resembling a giant, deformed skater.

At first the stone mounts moved at their usual slow pace, then suddenly, as the creature of pure evil began to rise, black saliva dripping from its jaws, the gargoyles shot forward, emitting a blast of pink fire and within seconds they were gone, leaving a trail of acrid smoke.

The creature rose above the tower, its head cocked to one side.

"Now what?" asked Damon, still shaken by the Pink Witch's terrible metamorphosis.

"Tell it to give chase," said Toshi.

"But what if it can't catch her – it – and ends up running wild for years?" asked Damon.

"Then command it to go somewhere where it can't bother anyone."

"But then someone else might find it and try and use it."

"They won't be able to without the Talisman," Toshi pointed out.

In the air a short way from where the monster lurked a dark patch appeared, like a small black hole and through it stepped Belinda. She jumped down onto the tower roof, backing away from the creature.

"Belinda!" called Damon and she looked up and gave a friendly wave.

"Hi there!" she called back. "Wynne called and told me what was happening"

"I have the Talisman!" shouted Damon. "What should I do?"

Belinda waved him down and Damon swooped towards her, Toshi close behind.

"I thought I'd use the second portal of the day to come and help you after all," said Belinda. "I wasn't entirely honest with you about my age and not being able to leave Misty Well. The truth is I was scared. The Pink Witch and I go back a long way, you see."

Damon glanced nervously at the creature, but it was making no attempt to harm anyone.

"You remember I told you the Pink Witch had a plain, not very talented sister?"

"Yes," said Damon.

"Well that was me," said Belinda. "I know so much about the Pink Witch and everything she did in that house because I was there for most of it. I stood by while she

347

starved her own children. I made some attempt to help them, but when she caught me and threatened to make me even uglier, I panicked and fled and by the time I returned they were dead."

A large tear popped from Belinda's left eye and crawled slowly down her cheek. "The whole set up at Misty Well is my way of trying to make up for being such a coward back then. And then when I was needed most, I acted like a coward again."

"You're here now," said Damon.

"And I really will make up for everything this time." She said resolutely. "I want you to command the creature to shrink to the size of a pea."

"What?" Damon stared at her, his top lip curled.

"Just do it," said Belinda.

Damon raised the Talisman. "I command the pure evil to shrink to the size of a pea!" he bellowed.

The monster craned its neck round to look down at him. Its face looked sad, realised Damon. And then with a strange noise, a little like the sound of air leaving a balloon, the creature began to shrink. It happened so fast, within seconds it was no bigger than Damon, crouched on the tower roof, looking up at him like an injured puppy. Seconds later and it was, as commanded, the size of a pea.

"Now what?" asked Damon, but Belinda pushed past him and plucked the tiny black creature from the ground.

"Now this," she said, popping it into her mouth and swallowing. She grimaced and let out a loud belch.

"Is that safe?" asked Damon. "What if it changes you like it did Wynne's mum?"

"I'll just have to hope there's enough good in me to cancel out the evil," said Belinda. "If not I'll take myself off somewhere remote and pass away my days where I can't hurt anyone.

Damon smiled. "That was either very brave or very stupid," he said.

Belinda grinned back at him. "We can discuss which on the way back to Misty Well," she said. "It will take a few days by horse and carriage."

Wynne came running towards them, flinging her arms around Damon. "You did it!" she cried.

"It was more Belinda than me," said Damon, blushing.

"And Toshi," said Wynne, stroking the large bird's head as he padded around them tutting.

"Would anyone like a cup of tea?" asked The Witch Mother from the doorway, and everyone laughed at the normality of such a question after such bizarre events.

"I could do with something to wash down that pure evil," said Belinda and she let out another loud belch.

EPILOGUE

The journey back to Misty Well took an entire day and night. They travelled in the Witch Mother's carriage, pulled by Barrow the horse. The time spent crammed in the box-like carriage gave everyone time to get to know each other better, and Wynne and her mother made good use of it. By the time Barrow plodded wearily into Misty Well, Belinda at the reins, they were closer than they had ever been and had decided not to return to the old house, but to start a fresh life somewhere far away from all the bad memories.

Kiskis was waiting at the entrance to the magic cottage as they approached on foot. He looked furious.

"Now is it time for me to go home?" he asked, arms folded across his scaly chest.

Belinda coughed and looked at the ground. "I'm terribly sorry," she said, "but I've led you on a bit where that's concerned. "I don't actually know how to send you back. No-one has used the well to travel between worlds for

351

centuries. It often went wrong, you see, particularly when people were trying to move their bodies across rather than their spirits. I think your people must have found their way through via a rip in the fabric between worlds rather than by magic. There are a few rips across Lightsleep, although their exact locations are unknown."

Kiskis scowled. "You let me think you could help me, just in case I could come in useful again. Didn't you?"

"Yes," admitted Belinda, looking embarrassed.

"So now I have to go off alone and look for some rip that may not even exist!" he stormed, slithering menacingly towards Belinda.

"No you don't," said Wynne, stepping between them. "You don't have to go alone. I'll come with you and I'm sure Damon and some of the others will too. You helped us so it's only right that we should help you."

"Really?" asked Kiskis, sounding unconvinced.

"Of course," said Wynne, "but first I need to sleep for a day or two."

"Me too" said Damon, not relishing the thought of another adventure so soon after the last one.

"Oh," said Kiskis. "That dirty man from the forest arrived with all the other children, a couple of giraffes and some tigers yesterday."

"Oh dear," sighed Belinda, "I don't know if I can cope with hundreds more. I do my best but even the magic of Misty Well doesn't give you endless energy."

"Maybe I could help," suggested the Witch Mother. "I said I wanted a fresh start, maybe this could be it."

"Maybe," said Belinda, guardedly.

"You could at least give me a chance…" began the Witch Mother, but then she let out a startled squeal. The dirty man from the forest had appeared behind Kiskis and was frozen in the cottage doorway, staring at the Witch Mother. "Mary," he said, his expression a mixture of fear and surprise.

"Bernard," said the Witch Mother, "is that you under all that foliage?"

"Yes, Mary, it is," replied the Forest Man.

"Wynne," said the Witch Mother, still staring at him, "I'm afraid this is your father."

2

Wynne had a lot to take in and decided to go to bed early to think about things. Damon asked if he could sleep in the bed beside Wynne's and Belinda created a small room for them to chat privately.

Damon waited outside while Wynne changed into a white cotton night-dress then climbed into his small, warm bed, wearing a large night-shirt made of the same cool material.

"Bit of a turn up for the books, your dad being the weirdo from the forest," he said.

"Yes," agreed Wynne. "I wonder how mum will take it. It was him leaving that helped tip her over the edge."

"Maybe things will work out between them," said Damon, yawning. And although he had meant to stay awake and chat with Wynne, he found himself drifting into much-needed sleep.

In his dream he was standing in a completely dark room, completely dark that is, apart from a spotlight which shone on the funny little man with the big head who had brought him to Lightsleep what seemed like months ago,

"Hello," said the funny little man. "It's time to go home."

"Really?" asked Damon. "Just like that?"

"Just like that," said the man. "We just needed to be sure of you. You are a special boy, Damon Dodge, and we couldn't take a chance on you turning bad. This adventure in Lightsleep is nothing to the task that lies ahead of you, a task only you and few others are qualified to take on. You've proved yourself worthy and one day I or one of the other In-betweeners will come back to you and explain everything more fully. For now you should return to your home and your mother and be a normal boy for a while – a normal boy who is a lot nicer than the one I met a few days ago, I hope."

"Please," said Damon. "Just let me say goodbye to Wynne."

The little man glanced at a large round watch face attached to his wrist by a piece of string.

"Be quick then," he said, "and then straight back to sleep so that I can swap you back over with the other Damon."

Damon woke with a start and found himself back in the small bedroom with Wynne still sitting up in the bed next to his, obviously deep in thought.

"Wynne," he said, sitting up himself, "I have to go back to my own world now. You'll get your real brother back again."

Wynne looked startled. "Really!"

"I expect that makes you pretty happy," said Damon.

"It will be nice to have him back," admitted Wynne, swinging her legs over the side of her bed. "But I'll miss you. You were fantastic destroying the pure evil and frightening the Pink Witch away."

"And you have been brilliant all along," said Damon. "I don't have a sister in my world, but if I did I'd want one just like you."

"Thanks," said Wynne and she hugged Damon tightly.

"I love you," whispered Damon, tears streaming down his face.

A scream reached them through the echoing halls of the magic cottage.

"That sounded like Joe," said Wynne.

"Don't worry," said Damon, "he's just found the big black beetle I put inside his bed."

"Damon!" scolded Wynne.

And then Damon sat up in his own bed in his own home and saw his real mother smiling down at him, a glass of orange juice in her hand.

"At last!" she said. "I thought you were about to wake up, you've been restless for a while now, groaning and muttering in your sleep."

357

Damon blinked away the remnants of his final goodbye with Wynne and grinned at his mother. "I didn't burn the house down then!" he said and his mother frowned.

"What are you talking about?" she asked, feeling his forehead. "Did you have a bad dream?"

"No," said Damon. "I was playing with the matches in your room and I set fire to the carpet. I'm so sorry."

His mother looked amazed at the word "sorry" coming from her son's mouth and felt his head again.

"You didn't set anything on fire," she assured him. "I found you sleeping on the floor in my room yesterday, next to my bedside cabinet. You were burning up with fever so I put you in bed and called out the emergency doctor. He said all I could do was keep you cool and give you lots of liquids. He came back yesterday and said your temperature had gone down. If he hadn't had good news I was going to take you into hospital. It was awful. Sometimes you'd wake up and stare at me like you didn't know who I was."

"I probably didn't," said Damon to himself and then out loud he said: "I love you, mum."

His mother looked concerned. "I think I'd better take you to hospital after all," she said. "Have a bit more sleep and we'll see how you are in an hour."

Damon laughed and lay back down. He did feel exhausted. And with his mother still looking down at him, a look of acute bafflement on her tired face, he fell into a deep, dreamless sleep.

Lightning Source UK Ltd.
Milton Keynes UK
UKOW05f0621100417

298756UK00016B/542/P